The
(She

Honoured with the sobriquet 'Gurudev', **Rabindranath Tagore** (1861–1941) was a Bengali poet, writer, musician and painter who single-handedly reshaped Bengali literature and music in the late-nineteenth–early-twentieth century. Tagore revolutionized Bengali art and literature by spurning rigid classical forms and remains to this day one of the most revered intellectuals in the history of Bengal. A dedicated educationist with no formal education, he also founded the Visva-Bharati University at Santiniketan. He was the first non-European to be awarded the Nobel Prize for Literature in 1913.

Dilip Basu is a professor at the University of California, Santa Cruz (UCSC), where he teaches history. He is the founding director of the Satyajit Ray Film and Study Center at UCSC. In addition to academic works on China, he is the author of *Satyajit Ray's Goddess—Devi* and the editor of the forthcoming collection of essays, *Mirrors of Modernity: The Cinema of Satyajit Ray.*

Dinkar Kowshik (1918–2011) was the dean at the Kala Bhavan in Santiniketan between 1967 and 1978 where he was earlier a student studying art with Nandalal Bose and Benode Behari Mukherjee. He was an eminent artist, art critic and art historian.

The Last Poem

(Shesher Kavita)

Rabindranath Tagore

Translated by
Dilip Basu

Illustrations
Dinkar Kowshik

HARPER**PERENNIAL**

NEW YORK • LONDON • TORONTO • SYDNEY • NEW DELHI • AUCKLAND

HARPER**PERENNIAL**

First published in India in 2011 by Harper Perennial
An imprint of HarperCollins *Publishers* India
a joint venture with
The India Today Group

Translation copyright © Dilip K. Basu 2011
Illustrations copyright © Dinkar Kowshik 2011

ISBN: 978-93-5029-123-8

2 4 6 8 10 9 7 5 3 1

HarperCollins *Publishers*
A-53, Sector 57, Noida 201301, India
77-85 Fulham Palace Road, London W6 8JB, United Kingdom
Hazelton Lanes, 55 Avenue Road, Suite 2900, Toronto, Ontario M5R 3L2
and 1995 Markham Road, Scarborough, Ontario M1B 5M8, Canada
25 Ryde Road, Pymble, Sydney, NSW 2073, Australia
31 View Road, Glenfield, Auckland 10, New Zealand
10 East 53rd Street, New York NY 10022, USA

Typeset in 12/14 Adobe Jenson Pro at
SÜRYA

Printed and bound at
Manipal Technologies Ltd., Manipal

In Loving Memory of
Dinkar Kowshik

Contents

1

Concerning Amit

AMIT RAY IS a barrister. His surname 'Rai' is usually spelt 'Roy' or 'Ray' in English, robbing it of the elegance of the Bengali spelling. Amit joined the multitude of others bearing that surname. Aspiring to be different, Amit spelt it in such a way that he soon became Amit Raiye to his English friends.

Amit's father was also a barrister, a famously successful one. He had amassed a huge fortune—enough to feed and support the prodigal lifestyles of three generations of Rays.

Amit left for Oxford without finishing his studies at Calcutta University. He spent seven years at Oxford, but he refused to study at all—he was too intelligent for that. He read very little or nothing, but this was not apparent to his peers, who were impressed by his ready tongue and wit. His father had expected nothing extraordinary from his son; all he desired was that the Oxford polish Amit had acquired stay fast even back home in Calcutta.

I like Amit. He is a smart chap. I am a young writer, with only a few who care to read my books—Amit is the most able reader of the lot. He admires the flair of my writing. He condemns the well-known, popular writers of our country as having no style or class. He compares them to a camel, uncouth and clumsy, walking awkwardly through the barren, faded, desert-like landscape of Bengali literature. I must hasten to add that this is Amit's opinion, not mine.

Fashion may be the mask, says Amit, but style is the face upon which it must be worn. Style belongs to those few writers who have a mind of their own, and fashion is the forte of the mindless many whose only job is to please the multitudes. Bankim's style is apparent in his famous novel *The Poison Tree*; the Bankim fashion or a fad is evident in Nasiram's opus *Manamohan's Marvels*—there, Nasiram revels in purple prose, but really murders Bankim's style. One can watch the garishly clothed nautch girl at a public show, but one requires a scarf of fine Benares silk to cover the head of a beautiful bride at her wedding. The garish clothing is fashion; the scarf of Benares silk is style. Because people are afraid to stray from the beaten track, they scrupulously avoid style in our land, says Amit. The Puranic tale of the famed sacrifice of King Daksha is a case in point. All the fashionable high gods like Indra, Chandra and Varuna received their gold-embossed invitations, but Lord Shiva was an original, so original that the presiding priests at

Amit Ray

the sacrifice considered it inappropriate to invite him. I enjoy hearing such outlandish talk from an Oxford man, for I believe my writings have style—which is why they all attain nirvana without the fear of a rebirth: the first edition is also the last edition.

Navakrishna, my wife's brother, cannot stand Amit and his airs. 'To hell with that Oxford man,' he exclaims. He himself is an MA, with excellent marks in English literature; he has vast learning, but little understanding. The other day, he told me scoldingly, 'Amit extols the virtues of unknown writers to make fun of the great masters. He loves to beat his own drum, and you are his drumstick.' Unfortunately, this was said when my wife was present. It is good to record that she didn't like what her brother had said. Although she had had a negligible education, she seemed to share Amit's views. Women have wonderful natural instincts.

Sometimes, I too wonder when Amit cavalierly dismisses well-known English authors. Such authors are hot property in the book market. One doesn't need to read them to admire them. One has to only praise them highly to earn good marks in examinations. Amit too doesn't need to read them to revile them. In truth, the famous authors are public property, like the waiting room at Burdwan station; the authors discovered by Amit are his special reserve, like the saloon car in a special train.

Amit is obsessed with style. It is not limited to his literary choices; it extends to his dress, manners and personality. He stands out in any crowd: one and one only! His full frame is accompanied by a clean-shaven, dark face, playful smile and manners, expressive eyes and a restless gait. He doesn't take even a moment to respond to things; his retorts are fast and swift. He generally wears Bengali outfits for the simple reason that it is not fashionable in his social set. His dhoti is carefully crinkled and borderless. Ordinarily, young people don't wear borderless dhotis, and that is precisely why Amit wears it. His kurta is buttoned down from the left shoulder to his waist on the right, and the seams of his sleeves are wide open from the cuffs to the elbows. He wraps around his waist over the dhoti a broad, maroon, gold-embroidered sash; on its left hangs a small bag made of Vrindavan chintz, which he uses to keep his pocket watch. He wears on his feet a pair of red-and-white slippers made in Cuttack. When he goes out, a south Indian chaddar, neatly folded, hangs from his left shoulder down to his knee. When invited out, he flaunts on his head a white, embroidered Islamic cap. The whole thing is a show. His English outfit is equally absurd, but those who are familiar with London fashions say that the loose clothing Amit wears is considered 'distinguished'. He doesn't wish to make himself look outrageous; all he wants is to ridicule what is in fashion. There are plenty of young men who try their hardest to look young; Amit's youthfulness requires no certificate. It is extravagantly obvious, beaming with its spontaneous natural splendour.

Amit has two younger sisters—Cissie and Lissie. They are the best imports of the latest brand of high fashion, smartly packaged, from head to toe, like showroom exhibits. They wear high heels and dangle through their open jackets strings of amber and coral beads; they wrap their saris tightly around their curves. They trip when they walk; they speak in high-pitched voices; they laugh loudly; tilting their heads, they cast sidelong glances. Rose-coloured silk fans flutter at their cheeks; sitting on the arms of chairs of their male friends, they flirt, expressing mock anger at pretended passes.

Amit's popularity among such fashionable young women in his social circle is a matter of envy among men. But Amit remains somewhat indifferent, showing favour to none of them in particular while being warm and amiable to all. He pretends he is not bowled over by women while maintaining his interest in their company. Amit attends parties, plays cards, loses bets willingly; he implores the woman who is a bad singer to sing again. If he meets a young woman wearing a loud-coloured sari, he asks her to name the store where she bought it. When he meets a young woman for the first time, he shows immediate interest, even though his friends know this is just a pretence. It is as if someone who worships many gods privately tells each one of them he is the greatest. And so the daughters, their mothers still clinging to hope, realize that Amit is like a sliver of light in the horizon that isn't going to brighten their lives or really give them any hope while pretending to extend it. His mind argues about women endlessly without ever coming to a conclusive decision. He is friendly to everyone without being intimate; his charm and warmth are like sparks that do explode.

The other day, at a picnic, Amit sat beside Lily Ganguly on the bank of the Ganga; the moon rose above the deep dark sky on the other side. Amit softly whispered to Lily, 'The new moon is on the other side, you and I on this— this priceless moment will not return.' At first, Lily was elated. Soon, she realized these were just words, just as illusory as the riot of colour on a bubble. She pulled herself out of the momentary delusion and giggled. 'Amit, what you say is so obvious that you didn't need to say it at all. Just a moment ago, a frog plopped into the water— that moment too will not return.'

Amit replied, smiling, 'There is a difference—a vast difference. At this time of the evening, the jumping frog is immaterial. You, I, and the moon, the endless ripple of the river and the millions of stars in the sky, have a certain harmony, like Beethoven's *Moonlight Sonata*. It is as though the architect of the world had designed a lovely gold ring wrought with diamond, emerald and sapphire, but no sooner had he finished making the ring than it dropped into a vast ocean where no one could find it.'

'Just as well, Amit. The creator of the ring will not send you a bill.'

'But Lily, imagine a million years later, in the shadow of the golden glow of Mars, on the shore of a vast lake, we meet again. As in Kalidasa's *Shakuntala*, a fisherman cuts open the fish, and a ring of recollection pops out, and we get back the wonderful golden moment of this evening. What would happen then?'

Lily stroked Amit with her fan. 'Then the golden moment will drop again in the ocean and disappear. Many such precious moments have passed you by. You have not kept count.'

Cissie and Lissie

She then got up and joined her friends. This is a sample of innumerable such episodes of Amit's encounters with young women.

'Why don't you get married, Amit?' asked his sisters Cissie and Lissie.

'The first thing in the wedding is the bride, next is the groom.'

Cissie replied, 'You shock me, Amit. Don't we have an abundance of suitable brides?'

'In the past, a bride was chosen based on her horoscope,' Amit retorted. 'I want one who doesn't need a horoscope, who is unique, without a peer!'

'When she joins you in marriage,' said Cissie, 'she will take a second place to you, right?'

'The bride of my imagination is without an address. She is like a meteor from the sky, gone before she can enter a home.'

'In other words, she is not like any of your sisters!' fumed Cissie.

'In other words,' Amit affirmed, 'she will not come as a mere addition to the family.'

'Isn't Bimi Bose enamoured of Amit?' Lissie asked Cissie. 'She is just waiting for a nod from Amit. Why doesn't he like her? He says she lacks culture. Why so? She has a master's degree in Botany—she stood first in her class! She is obviously a learned scholar. Isn't that so?'

'Learning is like a stone,' said Amit, 'culture is the sparkle. One has weight, the other has shine.'

'Listen to him!' Lissie exploded. 'Bimi Bose isn't good enough for him! As if he is good enough for her! I'll warn

Bimi not to look at Amit again, even if he begs to marry her.'

'Unless I go crazy, why would I marry Bimi Bose? If I ever agree to marry her, don't organize my wedding— send me to a lunatic asylum instead!' retorted Amit.

Amit's family and friends have given up on his prospects for marriage. They are convinced that he doesn't want the responsibility that comes with marriage, that he only dreams impossible dreams and shocks people with his unorthodox opinions and views. His mind moves like lightning: it is too sharp and quick. He is not suited for mundane household duties and responsibilities.

He whiles his time away, entertains near-strangers to tea at Firpo's, takes his friends out for long drives at odd hours of the day, goes on buying sprees and gives away what he buys to complete strangers. He buys expensive English books published abroad, and then leaves them at friends' homes, forgetting to collect them back.

What drives his sisters mad is his contrary personality. In a polite social gathering, he is sure to say something that will scandalize everyone. One day, he cut short a political scientist discoursing on the merits of democracy, stating, 'When Vishnu cut Sati's lifeless body with his discus, a hundred or more sacred spots sprung up wherever her dismembered limbs had fallen. Democracy today is like the scattered aristocracy. Petty aristocrats have popped up all over the world: we have political aristocrats, literary aristocrats and social aristocrats. All of them are ciphers, good-for-nothing, for not one of them believes in himself.'

Another day, as a feminist advocate was critiquing male

domination over women, Amit interjected: 'Once man ceases to dominate, the will of women rules. Despotism of the weak is dangerous.'

All the women and feminists present angrily demanded: 'What do you mean?'

Amit responded, 'Those who are in power shackle their victims in chains; but those who have no chains dement their victims with drugs. In the first case, victims are shackled but not demented; in the second, they are at once chained and demented. Women's purses carry drugs, and Nature's devilry keeps up their supply.'

Yet another day, at the Ballygunge Literary Society, the subject of discussion was the poetry of Rabindranath Tagore. For the first time, Amit had agreed to chair the meeting, fully prepared to battle the literary pundits present. The main speaker belonged to an older school: he elaborated with great erudition why Tagore's poetry was wonderful. With the exception of one or two people, all agreed. It was then the chair's turn to speak.

'A poet must not exceed a five-year tenure to write, say, between the ages of twenty-five and thirty. From the succeeding younger generation, we shall demand not just something better but also something which is different. When the mango season is over, we don't look for mangoes; rather, we demand big and fresh apples. The green coconut lasts only a short while, its milk evaporates; the ripe coconut lasts long, its kernel endures. Poets are ephemeral, necessarily young, while philosophers are ageless. The strongest objection to Tagore is that he, like old Wordsworth, keeps writing poetry well past his middle age. Many a time, the messenger of Death has called on him, but he holds on to the arms of his chair, refusing to call it a day. If he doesn't quit, it is our duty to quit his court en masse.

'The one who will succeed him will enter in triumph, bragging that his innings has begun with spectacular fireworks. For a time, his aficionados will fete him, adore him—until the auspicious hour of sacrifice will arrive, and he too will have to go and be bid adieu. This is the way the four-footed god is worshipped in Africa. This is also the way the two-footed, three-footed, four-footed and fourteen-footed gods of metre should be worshipped. No desecration compares to the profanity of withholding recognition of creative work before it becomes trite. However, admiration and adoration also follow an evolutionary process. If what was admirable five years ago continues to occupy the same position today, it is obvious it is blissfully unaware that it is no longer alive. It needs a little push to prove that its sentimental followers have delayed giving it a fitful burial for fear of acknowledging its legitimate new successor. I have vowed to expose this shameful conspiracy of the Tagorites.'

Our Manibhushan adjusted his glasses and asked, 'Do you wish to abolish loyalty from literature altogether?'

'Absolutely. The age of poet laureates is over. My second objection to Tagore is that his works are like his handwriting—rounded or wary like the face of the moon or of a female. This is primitive, a copy of the patterns on Nature's palm. We expect the new laureates to produce works that are straightforward and sharp like a thorn or an arrow or a spear—not flowing but like a flash of lightning, like the pain of neuralgia, like a Gothic church, not like the architecture of our temples. I don't mind if they look like a jute mill or a government secretariat. Forget the sappy old rhymes; grab the new, like Ravana's abduction of Sita. If one cries and wails, give him no sympathy. If a Jatayu rushes in to the rescue, let him meet his end. Sooner or later, the monkeys of the land of Kishkindhya will be roused, a Hanuman will swoop down on Lanka, setting it on fire, and set the clock back. We will celebrate reunion with Tennyson, shed tears on Byron's neck, ask Dickens to forgive us for abusing him for a while, as we were under an evil spell. From the time of the Mughals till today, had the dream-architects built bubbles of marble domes all over this ancient land, all decent men over the age of twenty would have embraced renunciation and retired to the forest. One has to get out from under the spell of the Taj Mahal in order to appreciate it.'

This reporter must hasten to add that he found Amit's logic incomprehensible as his head was spinning. The report is even more difficult to understand than Amit's speech. The bits and pieces that I could salvage are presented here in an order that makes some sense.

Amit's vandalism of the Taj Mahal prompted one Tagorite to interject with a flushed face: 'The more good things we have, the better for us.'

'Quite the opposite. The good things are good because there are so few of them. The poets who are past sixty or seventy and are still shamelessly turning in their shoddy products only add to their cheapness. Self-plagiarism soon leads to mediocrity. For this reason, it is incumbent on the readers not to let these old imbeciles live any longer—I mean poetically, not physically. Let them linger on as experienced politicians, experienced professors and critics.'

A man who had asked a question earlier enquired, 'May we know the name of your new poet laureate?'

'Nivaran Chakravarti!' Amit quickly replied.

'Nivaran Chakravarti? Who is he?' came a chorus of surprised voices.

'Today, this question is like a little seed,' answered Amit. 'Tomorrow the answer to it will grow into a mighty tree.'

'In the meantime, we want a sample.'

'All right! Listen.' Amit pulled out from his pocket a long and narrow notebook and began reading out.

⌘

> *Here on earth*
> *Today, I bring up*
> *An unknown name*
> *To a known crowd.*
> *I am a stranger*
> *An object of curiosity to the crowd.*
> *Open the door!*
> *I carry a message*
> *In obscure letters*
> *From the Lord of Time:*
> *'Who are the brave*

Who will dare give Him
With the vow to die
An appropriate reply
To his daring question?'

They won't listen—
The army of fools
Puts barriers on the road.
Failed anger
Howls and screams
As it builds up in the chest
Like the torrents of ocean waves
Flushes the rocky shores
With the wish to die.

I've no garlands of flowers,
My chest is bare
I've no armour, no uniform,
Only a deep victory dot
Shines on my forehead,
I'm a poor man in rags
About to plunder your wealth.
Open all your doors
I've extended my palm
Whatever you wish to give me
Give me now.
You're all shaken up,
And scared,
You shout out loud,
'Go back right now
You're a scary beggar
Your loud scream

Shatters the world
In the middle of the night.'

Bring out your weapon
Stab me in my heart
Let death kill death
I'll sacrifice my life.
Chain me tight,
Cut up all my limbs
Without blinking an eyelid,
Your freedom is within my freedom.

Bring out the Shastras,
Hit me hard
Let the Pandits
Argue out loud
The meaning of the Message.
The power of words
Will force open the eyes.

Light the fire!
What is good today
May turn bad tomorrow,
If it reduces it to ashes
Let it be.
In my trial of fire
The world will achieve
A wondrous enlightenment.

My inscrutable message
Will shatter its dialectical opposition,
Shaking it root and branch.
My maddening dance

Will liberate those who want to be free,
Will feed the hungry,
Will water the earth,
Celebrate the unknown name.

⁓⁓⁓

This silenced the Tagorites, but they warned that they would convey their views in writing.

When Amit was driving home after confounding the assembly, Cissie remarked, 'You planned the whole thing to make a fool out of everybody, and carried your invention—Nivaran Chakravarti—in your pocket.'

Amit replied, 'To announce the coming of the unknown is the work of the herald. I am that herald. Today, Nivaran Chakravarti has arrived on earth. No one can stop him now.'

Cissie is secretly very proud of her brother. She asked, 'Amit, do you wake up every morning and plan every witty thing you are going to say that day?'

Amit replied, 'To be ready for all possibilities is the way of the civilized. To be caught unawares is for the unenlightened. Even this has been jotted down in my notebook.'

'You really don't have your own opinions. You always say what sounds clever at that particular moment.'

'My mind is a mirror. If I wrap it up with my set opinions, it will not capture the reflection of each fleeting moment.'

'You'll spend your whole life wrapped up in reflections,' said Cissie.

2

The Crash

AMIT DECIDED TO go to Shillong for the summer.
One reason he picked Shillong is that no one from his
circle of family and friends ever went there; the other was
that the hunt for suitable young men was not very keen
there. Cupid usually aimed his arrows in other fashionable
towns, not in Shillong. Amit's sisters shook their heads
and said, 'You may go there if you wish to; we won't join
you!'

Dressed in fake Persian shawls, carrying fetching little
parasols, his sisters went to Darjeeling. Bimi Bose was
already there. When she saw the sisters arrive without
Amit, she realized that in the crowds of people in
Darjeeling, the man she had longed to see wouldn't be
present. Amit had declared he was not going to Shillong,
camera in hand, like a typical tourist; he was headed there
to enjoy solitude.

He spent the first few days reading books under the shade of deodars. He didn't carry works of fiction, for reading novels while on a holiday was the pastime of most vacationers. He was reading Suniti Chatterjee on linguistics, hoping to find loopholes in his theory on the development of the Bengali language. In between strolls in the hills and forests and forays into linguistics, he decided that the beautiful landscape alone wasn't sufficient. It was like a tedious raga repeating itself to no end. He was as restless and frustrated here as he was in Calcutta. He thought of travelling to the plains of Sylhet and Shilchar just to avoid the hills of Shillong. Just around then, the monsoons arrived and the downpour drowned every hill and every tree in the town and country. It was reported that at Cherrapunjee the mountain ranges acted as a barrier against the onslaught of ceaseless showers, that soon the waterfalls would overflow and overwhelm the ranges. Amit decided to shut himself up for a few days in a bungalow in Cherrapunjee. As in Kalidasa's classic *Meghaduta*, the cloud messenger flashed through thunder and lightning without leaving the name and address of the heroine.

He put on his woollen Highlander stockings, heavy boots, a khaki Norfolk jacket over shorts and a pith hat. He didn't look like the yaksha in the Kalidasa classic as drawn by Abanindranath Tagore, the famed artist. He looked like the district engineer out on road repairs—but he carried with him the pocket editions of poetry in several languages.

The road to Amit's house was narrow and crooked; on

its right was a precipice overgrown with shrubs. No traffic was expected. Amit was driving his car carelessly. He decided that, in these modern times, the motor car was appropriate for carrying the message to his beloved; as in Kalidasa's *Meghaduta*, there were the right measures of smoke, water, air and spark in the automobile to turn it into a motor messenger. If the driver carried a note, the message would be loud and clear. He decided that on the first day of the next rainy season, his car would follow the course described in *Meghaduta*. Who knows? He might meet an Avantika or a Malavika, or a Himalayan nymph— the heroines in Kalidasa's epic poem. Just then, as he navigated a curve, he saw a car approaching from the opposite direction. There was no room to pass. Amit put his foot on the brakes, but before he could stop, the other car crashed into his. There was a collision, but no one was hurt. The other car rolled down the hillside and stopped.

A young woman slipped out of the car. She looked like a figure etched by lightning, shining luminously. To Amit it was as if the Goddess Lakshmi had risen from the ocean which the gods had churned and stood calm and still among the foaming and raging waters. He looked at her in this rare moment. Had he met her in a Calcutta living room among a dozen other women, he might have noticed her, but he would have missed the special circumstance of meeting her here and now. One can meet many people in the world who are worth meeting, but rarely in the right place.

She was wearing a white sari of fine woollen fabric, with a narrow border, and white leather shoes. She was

Shillong

Accident

tall and slim, had a light brown complexion, large eyes with thick lashes, and her long hair was tied back in a knot. She was wearing a long-sleeved jacket, and two plain bangles on her wrists.

Amit left his hat in the car and stood in front of her quietly, expecting her to chastise him. The young woman seemed amused. He managed to mumble, 'I'm sorry.'

She smiled. 'There's no need to apologize. It was a mistake, and it started with me.'

She spoke gently and softly; it sounded like the smooth voice of a young boy.

When Amit returned home, he racked his brains for a word to describe her voice. It seemed to have a quality of its own. He wrote in his notebook: 'Her voice floats like the smoke of scented tobacco in the hookah, mellowed by its passage through water, cured of the acrid taste of nicotine, with the subtle aroma of the rose.'

But in the here and now, the woman, apologizing, added, 'I was going to meet a friend who I had heard had come to town. After driving some distance, my chauffeur said it was the wrong way. But it was impossible to turn the car, so we were going ahead anyway when your car crashed into ours.'

At this point, the chauffeur reported that although the car was not badly damaged, it would take some time to repair.

'If you would kindly pardon my guilty car, I would like to give you a ride to wherever you wish to go,' said Amit.

'No need, thanks. I'm used to walking up and down these hills.'

'I need to just to prove to myself that you have pardoned me.'

The woman hesitated. Amit said, 'I have something more to say. I drive—it's nothing special, you can't reach unto posterity driving a car. We met through this unfortunate accident—just give me a chance to show that I'm as worthy as your chauffeur.'

Women are wary of strangers, worrying about possible dangers. However, the ice seemed to have already been broken: the two had met on the quiet mountain road. It was as if they were destined by Providence to meet.

Without further word, the woman got into Amit's car. They reached her home. 'If you have time tomorrow, please drop by. I will introduce you to my foster mother.'

Amit wished to say he had plenty of time at hand, he could come in right then and there. But he felt he shouldn't.

Returning home, he turned to his notebook and started to write: 'What a crazy thing happened today on the road! It brought together two of us and launched us on the same course through the collision of two cars. The astronomers are wrong. It was from an unknown sphere that the moon moved into the earth's orbit. Our cars collided as if we had been walking the same path age after age, our faces shining, the bond between us never broken. Deep down, I feel our journey has begun—hand in hand, we will thread together the flowers of our garland. Our chance encounter is as sudden as it is momentous.'

It was raining. Walking up and down his porch, Amit broke into a silent invocation. 'Where are you, Nivaran Chakravarti? Come to me, give me words, give me a voice!'

Out came his notebook, and Nivaran Chakravarti dictated a poem.

❧

We're set on an unbound road
Without end.
The moment of our meeting
Explodes in a riot of colours
On the horizon.
The rains pour
And the lightning
Dances on the horizon
To the delight of our hearts.

We don't need baskets of flowers,
Nor a spectacular grove in the garden.
An unknown flower blossoms
In the morning light
Over the groves of rhododendrons.

We don't have inherited wealth,
Nor the love and care of family.
We're here like a pair of free birds
Outside a cage
Basking in the shining light
Of the unthinkable.

❧

Let us go back a little at this point and provide the background details.

3

Background

JNANADASHANKAR WAS CAUGHT in the storm of the radical upsurge against tradition that marked the introduction of Western education in Bengal. He belonged to the older generation, but was taken in by the new wave of change. He was ahead of his time. He wasn't like his contemporaries. He was like a seabird frolicking on the waves, defiant and fearless.

Two generations down the line, his grandson Varadashankar was his polar opposite. After his father's sudden death, he attempted to return to the ways of yore. He worshipped the serpent goddess, as well as the goddess of smallpox. He would spend the morning reciting the thousand names of Goddess Durga, drinking the sanctified water after washing his sacred amulet with it. He waged wars against the pretensions of non-Brahmins to acquire knowledge; with the support of learned Pandits, he lashed

Yogamaya

out against the upstarts who promoted modern science and rationalism. He fortified himself by practising strict penance and piety. At the age of twenty-seven, after rigorously worshipping the sacred rituals daily, he passed on.

His widow Yogamaya was the daughter of Varada's father's college classmate Ramlochan. Together in their radical days, the fathers of this wedded pair had eaten forbidden food in foreign restaurants. At that time, there was no conflict between Yogamaya's in-laws and her own parents.

The young women in Yogamaya's father's household were educated and followed no purdah; they travelled, even wrote illustrated travelogues for publications. After the death of his father-in-law, Yogamaya's husband set out to cleanse her completely of these modern contaminations. Her movements were strictly restricted, her head was covered with a veil. The Goddess of Learning was banished from the house, her English literature books were confiscated; only the Bengali works published before the era of Bankim were allowed. A Bengali translation of *Yoga-Vashistha Ramayana*, a deluxe edition, adorned the shelf. Till his last day, the master of the house fervently hoped that he would one day find time to study this timeless classic.

Yogamaya found it hard to swallow the ancient wisdoms that dictated her youthful iconoclasm. She escaped from her mental confinement in the counsel of the wise family priest Pandit Dinasharan Vedantaratna, who admired her natural and bright intelligence. He used to say, 'The rigmarole of such austere rituals is not for you! The foolish not only fool themselves, they are fooled by the whole world as well. Do you think we really believe in all this? Haven't you noticed we manipulate the Shastras to suit the convenience of the moment? It shows we have little faith in these silly rituals—we still perform them to satisfy incredulous believers. Since you don't want to be fooled, I can't fool you. Please call on me when you have questions. I shall explain to you the essential truth in our scriptures.'

Every now and then, he visited Yogamaya and expounded on what he believed to be the true meaning of the messages of the *Bhagavad Gita* or those of the *Brahmabhashya*. She asked intelligent questions, which delighted the pandit. He showed little respect for the spiritual instructors Varadashankar had around him. He told Yogamaya that she was the only one in town he enjoyed discussing the scriptures with. 'You have saved me from self-contempt,' he would say. Somehow, she managed to survive the regimen of strict rituals and fasts and empty scriptural injunctions.

After her husband's death, she lived a freer life with her son Yatishankar and daughter Surama. They spent the winters in Calcutta and the summers in the hills. Yatishankar was in college; Yogamaya couldn't find a suitable school for Surama, so she hired a private tutor for her. Her name was Lavanya, the woman whose car Amit had crashed into.

Avanish

Avanish and Lavanya

4

Concerning Lavanya

LAVANYA'S FATHER, AVANISH Datta, was the head of a college in western India. He took care of his daughter, who had lost her mother, the busy life of a college principal notwithstanding. Lavanya was a serious student; she remained intellectually and academically engaged even after graduation.

Learning was her father's passion, and this passion was transmitted to Lavanya in full measure. He loved his daughter more than all the books in his library. He believed that a person whose mind is deeply immersed in seeking knowledge need not get married, for all his desires would be fulfilled by the pursuit of learning. He believed that his daughter's intellect had reached a supreme level of sophistication—she didn't need a husband. If she had had any room in her heart for a potential partner in life, that space was already filled with her cultivation of the pursuit of history and mathematics. 'Let her remain married to knowledge and learning,' he concluded.

Shobhanlal was another object of his affection. It was rare to find a young man so completely devoted to his studies. His physical features were just as attractive: broad forehead, clear eyes, a genial curve to his lips, a sweet smile on his youthful, handsome face. He was, however, extremely shy. He became very nervous when people looked at him admiringly.

He came from a poor family and supported himself with scholarships and grants that he earned as an excellent student. Avanish was convinced that, one day, Shobhanlal would be a famous scholar, and the credit would belong to him as his mentor. Shobhanlal had free access to Avanish's library and to his intellectual guidance. But the sight of Lavanya made him nervous; he would always keep his head down to avoid eye contact with her. Lavanya ignored his presence; she had no use for a young man who lacked the self-confidence to face a young woman.

One day, Nanigopal, Shobhan's father, showed up at Avanish's home and subjected him to a volley of abuse. He alleged that the professor had laid a trap to lure suitable young men to his home under the pretext of tutoring them. He alleged that Avanish had plans to have Shobhanlal married to a woman belonging to a different caste to demonstrate his liberalism and commitment to social reform. As evidence, he produced a sketch of Lavanya, which he had found in Shobhanlal's suitcase. It was covered with rose petals. He had no doubt it was Lavanya's gift to his son. He had figured that Shobhanlal would command a substantial dowry in the marriage market, and that his value would rise further with the passage of time. Avanish had designs of getting such a valuable commodity gratis, Nanigopal alleged. It was nothing short of a daring daytime robbery—it was as good as stealing hard cash.

Lavanya was blissfully unaware that all this time she had had a secret admirer, that she had been placed on a pedestal. Shobhanlal had found an old photograph of Lavanya among Avanish's papers in his library. He had had a copy made for him by an artist friend and put back the photograph where he had found it. The roses, offered to the object of his secret, bashful love, were also from his friend's garden. Shobhanlal had to pay for this transgression. Wiping a secret tear, with a flushed face and his head down, he had to bid farewell to his professor's house.

In the BA finals, Shobhanlal topped the list while Lavanya was third on the list. For two reasons, the final results hurt Lavanya's pride. First, she resented Avanish's great admiration for Shobhanlal's intellect; second, the great affection that accompanied this admiration made Lavanya jealous of Shobhanlal. She had studied hard to get ahead of Shobhanlal in the final examination; when she learnt that he had outstripped her, she found it hard to forgive him. She credited Shobhanlal's brilliant success to her father's teaching. She had no hopes of doing better than him in the MA finals either. And yet, she did. Avanish was surprised. If Shobhanlal had been a poet, he would have written a volume of verse; instead, he deliberately yielded to Lavanya, allowing her to do better than him in the MA finals.

Around this time, Avanish suddenly heard the call of Cupid. Until now, romance had had no place in his life, which was filled with books and journals. He was forty-seven. At this vulnerable age, a widow entered his life, defying the books in his library and his complete dedication to scholarship. There was no bar against getting married except for his abiding love for Lavanya. He was distracted, his studies were neglected and he became completely absent-minded. There were books to review for journals. For example, he was asked to review an important book on the decline of Buddhism in India. He sat still in front of the book, ignoring the repeated calls of the editor.

One thing pricked his conscience: he had thus far not noticed that Shobhanlal was in love with Lavanya. He blamed himself as a father, and also Nanigopal. Shobhanlal was an obvious choice for Lavanya. Shobhanlal wrote to borrow some books on the Gupta dynasty; Avanish wrote back right away, inviting him to use his library as he had done in the past.

Shobhanlal was touched by the warmth of the invitation. He assumed it had the tacit approval of Lavanya. He started visiting Avanish's study regularly. He ran into Lavanya every now and then and hoped that she would speak to him, enquiring how his studies were progressing, show some curiosity about his interpretation of the Guptas. But not a word so far from Lavanya. And he didn't have the courage to inititiate a conversation with her.

Time passed. One Sunday noon, Shobhanlal was

Shobhanlal

browsing through a book, occasionally making notes. Avanish had left home saying he would not be back for tea in the afternoon. Suddenly, the door was flung open. Lavanya entered. Shobhanlal got up from his chair, unsure of what to say. Lavanya looked furious. She said, 'Why do you still come here? You know how your father insulted us.'

'Please forgive me,' Shobhan replied. 'I'll leave immediately.' He didn't mention that he came on her father's invitation. He collected his books and papers and walked out.

Lavanya was convinced her father was secretly nursing the hope that she and Shobhanlal would fall in love with each other. The very thought made her angry.

She insisted that Avanish marry the widow. Avanish had willed half of his inheritance to Lavanya. After he married, Lavanya refused to have any part of it. She said that she would find work and support herself. Avanish was hurt. He said that he hadn't wanted to get married, but had done so at Lavanya's insistence. Why then was she rejecting her inheritance? Lavanya responded, 'I don't want anything to affect our wonderful relationship, Father. Please do not worry. Just give me your blessings to make me happy.'

She got a job. It was as Surama's tutor—Yati refused to have a woman as his teacher. Lavanya remained busy. In addition to taking care of Surama's studies, she immersed herself in her own pursuits of ancient Greek and Roman history, perusing volumes written by Grote, Gibbon, Gilbert and Murray, and in reading English literature from ancient times to recent trends represented by George Bernard Shaw. It was not that she didn't think of other things in life once in a while, but these remained insignificant. It was around this time her car collided with Amit's.

It was a moment of self-discovery for her. 'Wake up Lavanya,' she said to herself.

Amit and Lavanya

5

Getting Acquainted

LAVANYA ASKED AMIT to wait in her study and went to fetch Yogamaya. Amit sat there and looked around. There were English literary works on the shelf, books Lavanya had obviously read. Books that she had read with keen interest, books that sat on her lap when her mind was distracted. He noticed that there was a volume of poetry by the English poet John Donne. While at Oxford, the works of Donne and his contemporaries had been the subject of Amit's critical study. By coincidence, the poetry of Donne would now draw them together—the very thought made Amit feel happy.

Gone were the days of drab and dull existence. The monotony of life, like reading an old textbook over and over again, will wear off, Amit mused. There had been no reason for him to look forward to the next day as it had promised to be the same as today. But now, in a moment, he felt transported to a different world. Here, everything seemed light, floating above the earth, everything moved steadily towards the improbable and inconceivable; the body was gently caressed by the breeze longing to play the flute, the light of the sky surged in every limb, the mind danced in ecstasy, casting off the dusty veil that had covered it. When Yogamaya gently walked into the room, this simple fact struck Amit with wonder. 'It is not that someone just entered, it is an advent,' Amit thought to himself.

Yogamaya was about forty, but her age didn't show on her complexion or face. She exuded a radiant glow, smiling gently. She was wearing an ordinary white sari that covered her close-cropped hair, as was the custom of a Hindu widow. She was barefoot. Amit touched her feet in respectful greeting.

Introductions over, Yogamaya said, 'Your uncle Amaresh was the best lawyer in our town. Once, someone had slapped a big lawsuit on my family, and he came to our rescue. He used to call me Boudi.'

'I'm his unworthy nephew,' Amit said. 'My uncle saved you from loss; I've caused you a loss. You were his Boudi—now you will be my Mashima.'

'Is your mother living?' Yogamaya asked.

'No, she has passed away. I'm without a mother,' Amit responded. 'I don't have an aunt either.'

'Why are you so interested in an aunt?' Yogamaya was curious.

'Allow me to explain. If I had smashed my mother's car, she would have been furious, scolding me for monkeying around with her car. But if it was Mashima's car, she would merely smile at my clumsiness, dismissing the matter as a childish prank.'

Yogamaya smiled. 'Well, so be it. Let the car be Mashima's.'

Amit sprang up, touched Yogamaya's feet and said, 'This must be the fruit of good karma. I was blessed with a mother, did nothing to pray for a Mashima. Smashing into a car can't be good karma—and yet, it has miraculously brought me a Mashima.'

Yogamaya smiled again. 'Fruit of whose karma? Yours, mine, or that of the auto mechanic?'

Amit passed his fingers through his thick crop of hair, pondering. 'That is a tough question, indeed. It's not one person's karma, it is the karma of the whole universe, from star to star, from age to age—someone has hatched a plot to work this, timed exactly at forty-eight past nine this Friday.'

Darting a sidelong glance at Lavanya, Yogamaya thought to herself: these two must marry. 'You two talk,' she said out loud. 'Let me make arrangements for lunch.'

Amit had the gift of quickly striking up a conversation. 'Mashima has asked us to talk, to get to know each other. The first thing one needs in an introduction is the name. Let this be the beginning. I suppose you know my name— what in English is called one's proper name.'

'All I know,' said Lavanya, 'is that your name is Amit Babu.'

'Not in all situations.'

Lavanya smiled. 'Situations may be many, but the name should be one.'

'What you are saying is rather old-fashioned—that there are differences in time and space, from one age to another, between men and women. To say that the name alone doesn't vary is unscientific. I've decided to become famous by advocating the relativity theory of names. But at the outset, let me clarify: to you, I'm not Amit Babu.'

'You prefer the English way, Mr Ray.'

'That comes from a far distance, imported from overseas. To measure the efficacy of a name, one must see how long the sound takes to travel from the ear to the heart.'

'What is that fleet-footed name?'

'To increase the speed, one must lighten the weight. Cut Babu from Amit Babu.'

'That is not so easy. It takes time.'

'Not for all. There is no such thing as *the* watch; the pocket-watch varies from pocket to pocket. That is Einstein's theory.'

Lavanya got up. 'The water for your bath is getting cold,' she said.

'I shall happily take a cold bath if you would stay here a little longer.'

'I'm sorry. I don't have time. There is work to do.' Lavanya left the room.

Amit did not go to take a bath right away. He tried to recall fondly how each word was emitted from Lavanya's mouth with a smile on her lips. Amit had met many beautiful women; their beauty was like the full-moon night, bright yet obscure. Lavanya's beauty was like the early morning star—there was no lure of mystery about it; her intelligence was evident and natural, she was sensitive and thoughtful. That is what fascinated Amit. He had intellect but no forbearance, a keen sense of discrimination but no patience, he was learned but had learnt no peace. In Lavanya's face, he saw serenity, calm and, above all, a balanced intellect and heart.

6

Getting Closer

AMIT IS BY nature social. He cannot sit still, admiring Nature's beauty. He likes to talk. One can't poke fun at forests and mountains, play pranks on them. They follow strict rules and expect the same of others. In a word, they have no sense of humour. That is why Amit likes the city, not the country. But now, a strange thing happened. The hills of Shillong seemed to have captivated him. Today, he rose before the sun, something contrary to his nature. Looking out of the window, he saw the sun rising beyond the hills in the distant horizon, shining golden rays through thin layers of clouds behind the deodar trees. The riot of colours in the sky was a sight to behold.

Amit gulped down a cup of tea and got out of the house. There was no traffic on the road. He sat on the thick carpet of fallen leaves of a pine tree. He lit a cigarette, but forgot to smoke it. The road led to

Yogamaya's house. Just like one savours the aroma of cooked food seeping out of the kitchen before one sits down to dinner, Amit was enjoying the glory of watching Yogamaya's house from this spot. When his watch would tell him that it was a respectable hour, he would go over there, announce himself and ask for a cup of tea.

He was expected in the evenings. Amit's literary expertise had earned him this standing invitation. On the first two or three visits, Yogamaya had joined in. But she soon realized that she was standing in the way—that three is a crowd and two is company. Since then, she excused herself on occasions. It became clear that these were not accidental but intended. Yogamaya recognized that there was something deeper in all this than literary pursuits. Amit realized that Mashima was older, but her mind was sharp. She knew what was going on, not just in literary discourse but deeper too. This encouraged him to propose that he would spend an hour in the morning and two hours in the afternoon coaching Yatishankar in English literature. He did it with such great enthusiasm that the mornings evolved into noons, the noons into afternoons. Lunch was inevitably included. His departure would then be delayed past dinner, of course.

His tutoring was supposed to start at eight in the morning. Normally, it would have been an unearthly hour for him. He was used to saying that the foetus in the mother's womb took ten months to grow—he could not adjust his sleeping hours to the measure of birds and bees. Till now, Amit's nights had encroached into his mornings. He would say that these stolen hours were so precious because they were forbidden. But these days, he was starting to get up early. He would wake up well before he needed to, and not remain in bed, lest he be late. Sometimes, he would push the time ahead on his watch to make sure that he was up before the appropriate time. Today, he looked at his watch and found that the hour was still on the wrong side of seven. Surely it had stopped! He put it to his ear and found it ticking.

As he listened to the tick-tock, he was startled to see Lavanya come down the road, swinging an umbrella in her right hand. She was wearing a white sari and carried a black shawl with fringed borders. He knew that Lavanya had noticed him, but was unsure about acknowledging it. As she reached a turning point, Amit could no longer restrain himself. He ran up to her.

'You knew you couldn't avoid me, so I had to run to catch up with you. It was embarrassing, you know.'

'How so?'

'The unfortunate one who lags behind wants to cry out loud. What name shall I use to call you? One good thing about gods and goddesses is that one can invoke them by their names. You can say "Durga! Durga!" and the goddess will not be displeased. But with your kind, it is different.'

'You might as well stop calling.'

'This may only be possible if you are within earshot. It would be more tragic if I wished to call you and yet was not able to call.'

'Why? I thought you were used to English ways.'

'Miss Datta? That's fine at the tea table. When the earth and the sky met in the light of dawn this morning,

Amit and Yati

the union celebrated the glory of heaven and earth; the call of heaven to earth, and earth to heaven. Can't such a moment occur in the lives of us mortals? Just imagine that I have, at this very moment, called out to you with all my heart and breath, and this call echoes from forest to forest and reaches the many-coloured clouds in the sky. The cloud-capped hills listen and brood over it. Can you imagine that name being Miss Datta?'

'It takes time to get used to a name. Let me finish my walk now.'

'It takes a while to learn to walk,' said Amit, staying by her side. 'But with, me it's different. It's only after coming here that I've learned to sit still. The rolling stone gathers no moss, as the saying goes. I've been sitting on the side of this road since it was still dark. I wanted to see the light of the dawn.'

'Do you know the name of the bird with the green feathers?' Lavanya tried to change the conversation.

'That there are birds in the world,' replied Amit, 'was commonplace to me until now. After coming here, I've had occasion to feel its special significance. I've learnt that there are birds and, what is more, that they sing.'

'How wonderful!' laughed Lavanya.

'You're laughing,' complained Amit. 'The problem with me is that even when I'm serious, my words don't sound serious. That is the curse of my life. The presiding heavenly body at the moment I was born was the moon. Even at the most hopelessly moonless night, she gives a flicker of a smile before fading away.'

'Don't blame me,' said Lavanya. 'Even the birds would laugh if they could hear you.'

Amit went on: 'You see, people laugh at my words because they don't grasp their meaning. If they did, they would pause to think. I'm saying today that I have discovered birds anew—even I can't laugh this away. There you are! You see, the words are the same, and you're now silent.'

Lavanya laughed. 'You're young, not ancient—rather, too new. Why then this passion for the newer still?'

'The answer is a profound truth which I dare not discuss at the tea table. What appears as new in me is also ancient—like this light of dawn, like this fresh lily, ageless, timeless, but discovered anew.'

Lavanya smiled and remained quiet.

'This smile of yours is like the light of a policeman's lantern shining on a thief. I know that you know where these lines are from, for these are from your favourite poet. Please, for heaven's sake, don't put me down as a plagiarist. There are moments when one transforms into a Shankaracharya and affirms that the difference between "I wrote it" and "he wrote it" is nothing but maya. Why, just this morning, I said to myself, let me pick out a line that only I could write. No other poet could have written it.'

'And could you pick one out?'

'Yes, I did.'

Lavanya couldn't restrain her curiosity. 'What is it?'

'For God's sake, hold your tongue and let me love!'

Lavanya was startled. After a long pause, Amit asked, 'You know who wrote it, of course?'

Lavanya nodded her head to indicate she did.

'The other day, I discovered a volume of the poetry of

John Donne on your table. Otherwise, this line wouldn't have occurred to me.'

'Discovered?'

'What else? One notices books in bookstores; on your table, they reveal themselves. Public libraries arrange their books on shelves; I saw on your desk that they receive tender, loving care. That day, I read Donne and he shook my heart. Other poets attract crowds; with Donne's poetry, two people can enjoy it sitting next to each other. So I could hear clearly what was in my heart.'

'*For God's sake hold your tongue and let me love!*' Amit said, translating it into Bengali.

'Do you write poetry?'

'I'm afraid I shall begin writing from now on. What the new Amit will do, the old Amit doesn't have the foggiest idea. Maybe he'll march to battle.'

'Battle? With whom?'

'That, I don't know. I just feel it. Soon, I must. I must stake out my life for something great, so that later I don't regret having missed the opportunity.'

Lavanya laughed. 'If you must fling out your life, fling it with care!'

'The warning is unnecessary. I don't just want to start a communal riot. I shall avoid the Muslims, avoid the British. If I run across an old fogey, looking grim and devout, driving his car and honking, I shall confront him and shout, "Do battle!" You know the type—one who is desperately ill, and instead of checking into a hospital, comes to these hills to take walks for the sake of one's appetite.'

'What if the old fellow totally ignores you? What then?' said Lavanya.

'Then I shall raise both my arms and exclaim: "This time around, I forgive you. You are my brother—both of us are the children of Mother India!" You know, when the heart expands and grows bigger, one both fights and forgives.'

Lavanya laughed again. 'When you were talking about a fight, I was alarmed. I'm now reassured that there is nothing to worry about as you are also talking about forgiving.'

'Will you do me a favour?' Amit asked.

'What is it?'

'Don't walk too far today to increase your appetite.'

'What then?'

'Let us sit under that tree next to that stream, on that rock which glistens with many-coloured mosses.'

Lavanya looked at her wristwatch. 'There is very little time.'

'That's the trouble in life, Lavanya Devi! There's only a half-pitcher of water to last through this path in the desert. One must make sure that the water doesn't spill in the sand. Those who have time to spare can afford to be punctual. The gods have plenty of time, and that's why the sun rises on time and sets on time. Our time is limited; for us to be punctual will be extravagant. Should someone from way above ask, "What have you accomplished in life on earth?" I would answer, totally shamed, "I was at work all this time, with my eyes fixed on the watch." That is why I plead, please join me over there.'

That someone could object to what he himself approved

was something Amit couldn't for a moment consider. This made it difficult for others to refuse him.

'Very well,' Lavanya yielded.

From the thick forest glade, a narrow path led to a Khasi village. A tiny stream from a waterfall flowed across it, past a bunch of little pebbles. That's where the two of them sat, by the side of a deep hollow where some water had collected. Lavanya blushed; she wanted to say something, anything, to mask her shyness, but nothing was said. To break the silence, Amit said, 'You know, there are two forms in our language—the literary and the colloquial. Besides the two, we should have a third, not for social or business purposes but for an intimate moment like this. Like the bird's song or the poet's lyrics, it should have a natural flow. The fact that we have to run to the bookstore to find that language is a matter of great shame. Just imagine going to the dentist every time we wanted to laugh. Won't you say something, Lavanya Devi?'

Lavanya remained quiet. Amit went on: 'At the tea table, one must distinguish between what is good form and what is not. But here, at this spot, neither is necessary. What to do? Perhaps one should recite a poem. If you would permit me, I shall begin.'

Lavanya granted him permission simply to avoid the discomfort of saying no.

'Do you like Tagore's poetry?' Amit asked.

'I do.'

'I don't. I have my own favourite poet. He is excellent, and that's why very few, if any, ever read him. I wish to recite one of his poems.'

'Why do you hesitate?'

'My experience has been painful. If one runs down a celebrated poet, he is ostracized. What I like, others may not. And that's why there are bitter battles among readers of poetry.'

'Don't expect a battle from me. I don't rely on others to decide what I should like or not like.'

'Well said. Let me then begin!'

O the unknown!
How will you leave me
Before I get a chance to know you?

'Please think of the subject—getting to know the unknown is a tough challenge. I'm locked up within the unknown; when I get to know it, I will feel free. This is the ultimate liberation.'

In the receding darkness
Of the moment when one wakes,
As the night breaks into dawn
I saw your face.
With our eyes sighting each other,
I asked, where have you been
Hiding in the unknown world
Of lost memory?

'One can't remain locked up like this, in the realm of the unknown, with no memory. We shouldn't give up in despair.'

~⊷⊶~

Getting to know you
Won't be easy.
Whispering softly into your ears
Will not do.
I shall win you over,
Conquering your doubt,
Your fear, your conflicted mind,
Bring you out to light.

~⊷⊶~

'Note its relentlessness, its power—the masculinity of its composition.'

~⊷⊶~

You'll wake in torrents of tears,
Will know yourself in a moment,
The bond will break,
Giving you freedom
I'll find my freedom.

~⊷⊶~

'You'll not find this kind of boldness in your celebrated poet. It's not just a lyric, it's like setting the sun on fire. It is a pitiless philosophy of life.'

Looking at Lavanya intensely, he recited:

O the unknown,
The day is done, the dusk sets,
Time will not stop.
Let the barriers fall,
Let the lights burn bright,
And let me throw in my life as an offering.

As he finished reciting, Amit held Lavanya's hand. She did not resist. She looked at him without a word. Words were not necessary. Lavanya forgot to look at her watch.

7

Match-making

AMIT WENT TO Yogamaya and said, 'Mashima, I'm here on a match-maker's mission. Please don't dismiss me outright.'

'First, let me have the name, address and a description.'

'You can't put a price tag on the candidate's name.'

'In that case, the match-maker's fee will be reduced accordingly.'

'That's not fair. The world of big-named people is wide on the outside and rather narrow on the inside. They are busy maintaining the grandeur of their life rather than its happiness. Such men can only spare a small fraction of themselves for their wives; this is not a proper marriage.'

'And what about his looks?'

'I can't talk about that, lest I exaggerate.'

'Exaggeration I suppose is the trick of your trade.'

'In choosing a groom, two things are critical—his name

must not outgrow the home, nor his looks outstrip his wife's.'

'All right, never mind the name and looks. What about the rest?'

'The rest is his worth. I can say he is not worthless.'

'Intelligence?'

'Enough to convince others that he has enough.'

'Learning?'

'It is like Newton's. He knows he is merely gathering seashells on the seashore of knowledge. Unlike Newton, he dare not say it in public, lest people take him at his word.'

'The list of the groom's qualifications seems rather modest.'

'To emphasize Annapurna's plenitude, Shiva agrees to call himself a beggar and is not ashamed of it.'

'In that case, make the name of the groom a little more explicit.'

'It is a known family. The groom's name is Amit Kumar Ray. Why do you laugh? I'm not joking.'

'I confess, my dear, I fear that the whole thing may turn out to be a cruel joke in the end.'

'This casts aspersions on the candidate.'

'It is no small achievement to keep one's life so light and full of laughter.'

'The gods have that power. That is why they are not fit for marriage. Damayanti knew that well.'

'Do you really like Lavanya?'

'How can I prove it? Give me a test!'

'There is only one test. You must be fully convinced that you wish to have Lavanya as the partner in your life.'

'Would you explain further?'

'That man is a true jeweller who recognizes the real value of the jewel, even though he may have bought it cheap.'

'Mashima, you are too subtle. It is like inserting a psychological twist to a short story. It is quite simple. A certain young man is crazy about a certain young woman and is keen on tying the knot. The young man is passable, and one cannot say enough about the young woman. Under the circumstances, most Mashimas in the world would start baking cakes to celebrate!'

'Don't worry about that. You want to wed Lavanya—all right. I'll know that you are worthy of her if you promise to continue to love her throughout your married life,'

'I thought I was ultra-modern—you have surprised me!'

'What is modern about it?'

'The twentieth-century Mashimas seem extra-careful about arranging marriages.'

'The reason is that the last century's Mashimas treated brides like dolls to play with. These days, those who marry are not interested in amusing Mashimas.'

'You need have no fear. One can never have too much in this world. Amit Ray has been born to prove this. Otherwise, why should my car, an insentient thing, crash into Lavanya's at that fantastic spot at that fantastic moment?'

'My dear, you don't sound grown-up enough to get married. You have some more growing up to do.'

'Mashima, my mind has a specific gravity of its own. That is why even when I'm serious, I sound light with my words. The heavy part lies unspoken in my heart.'

Yogamaya went in to arrange for lunch. Amit wandered

around from room to room, but couldn't find what he wanted to see. He came upon Yatishankar. He remembered that he had promised to read from *Antony and Cleopatra* with Yati that day. Looking at Amit, Yati realized that he must excuse himself from that chore that day—he felt pity for Amit. 'If you don't mind, I would like to take the day off and go hiking in the hills of Shillong,' he said.

Amit was overjoyed. 'One has to take a break from studies once in a while, otherwise what you study will not sink in. I don't mind if you wish to take the day off.'

'Tomorrow is Sunday. I'll be away from my studies, that's why I thought you'll mind if I ask not to learn my lessons today.'

'I'm not a schoolteacher. I don't like following a strict regimen, doing everything according to schedule. Enjoying a scheduled holiday is no fun—it's like hunting a tethered animal. It doesn't have the element of surprise, like when one is let go on a day that one is required to sit down for instruction.'

Yati thought it was funny the way Amit was all of a sudden waxing eloquent about the philosophy of holidays. He had guessed the real reason, and remarked, 'Lately, you have been preoccupied with the philosophy of holidays. The other day, you gave me a lecture on it. This way, I'll soon become an expert on how to go on unexpected holidays.'

'What did I say the other day?'

'You said that the inclination to do what one shouldn't is a great human virtue.'

Yati was in his early twenties. His realization that Amit was enamoured of Lavanya had put her in a new perspective to him. He had thought of Lavanya as a teacher; now, looking at her from Amit's standpoint, he realized she was a woman.

Smiling, Amit said, 'You have to be prepared when you have work to do—it should be inscribed in golden letters. On the other hand, it should also say that when you face the prospect of no work, you must take it as a challenge!'

'You seem rather excited these days.'

Amit patted Yati on the back. 'When you'll face the challenge of accomplishing work, do not hesitate for a moment.' Saying this, he left.

The roses were in bloom. There was a profusion of sunflowers in one corner, and chrysanthemums grew in square wooden pots. At the other end of the garden stood a tall eucalyptus. Lavanya sat beside it with her legs stretched out. The morning sun shone on her feet. There were bits and pieces of dry fruit on a handkerchief lying on her lap. She had thought of feeding the pets this morning, but had forgotten all about it. Amit stood beside her. She looked at him and smiled without saying a word. Amit sat down and faced her.

'Good news. I've got Mashima's consent.'

Without replying, Lavanya threw a walnut at the nearby peach tree. A squirrel slipped down its trunk.

Amit said, 'If you don't mind, I'll make your name shorter.'

'All right.'

'I shall call you Vanya.'

'You may call me by this name, but not around Mashima.'

'Of course. This will be meant for your ears only.'

'All right.'

'I too need an informal name. You decide what this will be.'

'I'll make yours shorter as well. I shall call you Mita.'

'Excellent! Why won't you call me by this name around everybody?'

'It'll then not remain special.'

'True. Vanya!'

'Yes, Mita?'

'If I write a poem, do you know what I would name it? *Ananya*.'

'What would that mean?'

'It would mean that you are you, not anything else.'

'There is nothing astounding about that.'

'How can you say that? It's astounding, very much so. Rarely does one run into another and is prompted to exclaim: "She is absolutely herself, unique, not like others." That's what I'll write in my poem.'

Vanya, you're unique!
Beautiful and blessed
By your own self.

'You will write this poem?'

'Of course I will. Who can stop me?'

'What made you so desperate?'

'I'll tell you. I was up till 2:30 in the morning, leafing through *The Oxford Book of Verse*. I didn't come across a single love poem I liked. It was clear I had to write one!'

Amit caught hold of Lavanya's left hand and grasped it between both his hands. 'My hands are tied! How shall I pick up a pen? The best rhyme is in the rhyming of hands ... Four fingers whisper into mine. No poet can express this so simply, yet so spontaneously.'

'You're so picky. Nothing ever satisfies you. This scares me!'

'Just consider my case. Lord Rama wished to test Sita's virtue by fire—visible, material fire. As a result, he lost her. The virtue of a verse also has to be tested by fire, but that fire must be of the mind. How is a man with no fire in his mind going to carry out that test? He will have to go by what others think, by hearsay. My mind today is all fire. By that fire, I'm reading again all that I've ever read. Very little of this survives. Most of it will burn to ashes. I must stand up in the company of poets, say the right word—say it gently and softly: "For God's sake, hold your tongue and let me love!"'

For a while, the two sat quietly. Lifting Lavanya's hand with his own, Amit pressed it gently over his face. He said, 'Just think, Vanya. At this particular moment this morning, innumerable people in the world desire something, but so few get it. I am one of the lucky ones. You alone have met this lucky man in the hills of Shillong, under this eucalyptus tree. The most wonderful things in life appear quietly, surreptitiously—so few notice it. Yet when a Tom, Dick or Harry shouts slogans from Goldighi in Calcutta to Noakhali or Chittagong, deals in dirty politics, everyone notices it. Perhaps it is just as well.'

'What is just as well?'

'None of the best things in life get any attention, yet they're in the primal consciousness of the world. Vanya! I'm talking away non-stop. You're quietly brooding. Tell me, what are you thinking about?'

Lavanya didn't respond. She sat there with downcast eyes.

'Your silence suggests that you're dismissing what I've said as worthless.'

Without raising her head, Lavanya replied, 'When I listen to you, I'm gripped with an unknown fear, Mita.'

'Fear of what?'

'What exactly you want of me, and how little I can give you, I'm at a loss to understand.'

'It is precisely because you can give without thinking. Your gift is precious!'

'When you said Mashima has given consent, fear seized me, fear of being caught and exposed.'

'Yes, caught you shall be!'

'Mita, your intellect is far superior to mine. While on the same road I shall fall behind, you'll look back at me. I shall not blame you. Please don't interrupt. Listen to what I have to say. Please do not marry me—trying to untie the knot will only add to the mess. What you've given me will stay with me till the end of my life. But please don't delude yourself.'

'Vanya, why are you worrying about tomorrow when we have plenty on our plates right now, today?'

Amit and Lavanya

'Mita, you've given me the strength to tell the truth. What I'm telling you now, you know in your heart that it is the truth. You just don't want to face it. You're not the kind to settle down. You're constantly seeking ways to satisfy your intellectual curiosity, flirting from one literary genre to another. I know that, in your heart, you consider marriage a vulgar thing. It is for those scripture-quoting, well-to-do folks who consider their wives as property to display in their living rooms along with their furniture.'

'Vanya, you're saying astonishingly harsh things with astonishing gentleness!'

'Mita, may I ever be tough in my love—let the power of love teach me to be completely honest with myself and not mislead you. You stay the way you are, don't take any responsibility that might detract you.'

'Let me have my say. Vanya, you have described my character correctly. I won't argue with that. But you're mistaken in one respect. Men change over time—there is a certain dynamism in their character, they are not like animals tied in chains. One day, the chain snaps, setting them free to roam the forest. They're then an altogether different sight!'

'What are you today?'

'The one that doesn't match my usual self. I've met many young women before socially, met them but not to get to know them. The strict parietal rules will not allow it. That's not the way we met, Vanya. We've got a chance to know each other.'

Lavanya remained silent.

'Let's say that there are two stars that encirle each

other, salaaming from a safe distance; they gravitate in a set pattern without ever meeting each other and break into fuming fire. This fire has changed Amit Ray completely. Vanya, you've lit that fire in me. We are no longer grinding in the motions of the everyday monotony of life.'

Lavanya's eyes were wet. She couldn't get rid of the thought that Amit's mind was essentially literary, every new experience rolled out a torrent of elegant phrases and words from his mouth. These were the harvest of his intellect and mind, not his heart. She had now warmed his heart but he didn't know how to show it. After a long silence, Lavanya suddenly asked: 'Don't you think the day the Taj Mahal was completed, Emperor Shahjahan was happy that his favourite and beloved queen Mumtaz had died? Her death was her greatest gift. The Taj reflects not Shahjahan's grief but joy.'

'Every moment,' Amit said, 'your words spring a surprise for me. You're a poet, no doubt.'

'I don't want to be a poet.'

'Why not?'

'I don't like to warm my life by lighting a lamp of words. Words suit those who set themselves up to organize world fairs or festivals. But my life's warmth is for the work of life.'

'You're denying the power of words, Vanya. You have no idea how you fire me up when you talk! I guess I have to call on Nivaran Chakravarti once again. You'll probably find him boring by this time. This fellow has the key to my heart. Nivaran's freshness is still intact, he refuses to become out of date. Each time he writes, it is as if it is his very first time. Rummaging through his manuscripts the other day, I came across a recent poem. It is on a waterfall. I wonder how he knew that I've discovered my waterfall in these hills of Shillong. He writes:

Waterfall, in the crystals
Of your flow,
The sun and the stars
See each other

'Had I written these lines myself, I couldn't have described you more vividly. The crystal-clear transparency of your mind illuminates your skin; in that light, I watch you, your smile and the words that come out of your mouth, when you're quietly seated and when you're walking down the road.'

Let the shadows swing and play
Upon your waters,
Let the shadows mingle
With the music of your laughter,
Give it a voice
The voice of eternity.

'You are the waterfall! You move with its stream. You speak as you move, the stones you step on break into melody.'

～～≈≈≈≈～～

My shadow, your laughter
Combine in one image.
The poet in me celebrates
In frenzy.
Step by step, in moment after moment,
The gleam of your light
Allows me to find words,
O Waterfall!
I can see myself in your stream,
I know myself.

～～≈≈≈≈～～

Lavanya smiled and said, 'For all my light and music, your shadow remains a shadow. It is beyond my powers to hold on to it.'

'One day, you'll see that if anything of mine survives, it will be my voice.'

'Where?' Lavanya laughed. 'In the archives of Nivaran Chakravarti?'

'Perhaps. The stream of my mind flows through Nivaran's fountain.'

'Then perhaps, one day, I'll find your mind in the fountain of Nivaran Chakravarti, nowhere else.'

At this point, the servant announced that lunch was ready.

As he walked, Amit pondered: 'Lavanya wants to analyse everything in my mind. She refuses to slip away in spontaneity, she won't give in. One exposes one's inner self, beliefs and convictions sometimes in life and writing—it moves, never stays still. Do I mix up life with writing? Is this where she differs from me? Is this the difference between man and woman? Man seeks plenitude in the powers of creative activity, forgetting his own self; woman uses all her energy in conserving, obstructing creativity, protecting the old? The two will inevitably clash, not unite. It seems that the highest fulfilment lies not in union but in freedom.'

These thoughts hurt Amit's feelings, yet he couldn't put them out of his mind.

8

Lavanya Argues

'LAVANYA, MY DEAR, are you sure you understand?'
Yogamaya said.

'Indeed I do, Mashima.'

'Amit is very restless, I agree. That's why I am fond of
him. He now looks distraught, as if everything is slipping
away from him!'

'If Amit was stable, if nothing slipped away from him,
he would be most unhappy. He lives by the dictum that
either he will not get what he is about to get, or he would
lose it as soon as he gets it. It is not in him to hold on to
something he already has.'

'To tell you the truth, that is what I greatly like in him.'

'That is the mother's indulgence and privilege. Mother
or aunt will indulge him, and he will enjoy the fun. But
why me? Why thrust it on me, the one who can't stand
it?'

'Haven't you noticed that he looks sad and subdued of late? I feel sorry for him. Say what you will, but he does love you!'

'That he does.'

'Then why worry?'

'Because I have no wish to be a tyrant and bring him to book.'

'All I know, Lavanya, is that love partly welcomes and partly practises tyranny.'

'Such tyranny must have limits. Where it is ingrained in one's personality, it overreaches itself. The more I read of love in literature, the more I am convinced that tragedy in love occurs when two people will not concede each other's individuality, where each strives to impose one's will on the other, where one attempts to mould the other in one's own image.'

'For that matter, it is hardly possible for two people to set up a family without some compromise, where one gives some and takes some. Where there is the bond of love, it shouldn't matter. Where there is no such bond, it leads to tragedy.'

'Leave out the person who is ready to settle down; he will make adjustments to make things happen. But the person we are discussing is made of altogether different stuff. He won't give up his unique personality and individuality. If a woman fails to realize this, the more she claims, the more she would lose her mate's love. I believe that, most often, what we call getting married is nothing other than putting handcuffs on one's hands.'

'What exactly do you want, Lavanya?'

'I don't want to get married to create unhappiness. Marriage is not for everybody. The fastidious pick and choose bits and pieces of an individual here and there. But once caught in the net of matrimony, man and woman are dragged too close to each other, with no room to manoeuvre. One can't maintain even a part of his or her individual self.'

'Lavanya, you really don't know your own self. It won't be necessary to reject any part of you.'

'But Amit doesn't want me. He has not noticed the everyday ordinariness in me, the girl at home. Whenever I say something simple, endless torrents of words start bubbling out of his mouth. He wants to refashion me with his words. When the words will fail him, he will notice the ordinary girl in me—the girl of his dreams will disappear. Marriage means acceptance—it leaves little to mould on the potter's wheels.'

'Do you think Amit won't be able to accept you completely?'

'If he can change his eccentric personality, he may have me. But why would he change? I don't want him to.'

'What is it you want?'

'Let me remain a dream in his imagination, wrapped up in his words, a plaything for his fancy. Indeed, why should I call it a dream? It is as if I've had a unique rebirth, a unique revelation of self in a unique world. What if it is only a colourful butterfly come out of its cocoon for a brief sojourn in this world? What is the harm if it rises with the sun and dies at sunset? What of it? All that matters is that this brilliant moment should not be in vain.'

'Very well. Let this encounter remain a momentary illusion. What about you? You don't wish to settle down at all? Will Amit always remain a shadow of an illusion?'

Lavanya became quiet.

Yogamaya broke the silence. 'When you argue out a case, I realize you're a learned, well-read person. But I've also seen the other side of you. The other night, around midnight, I saw the light in your room. I looked in. I saw you at your desk, holding two books in your lap, and you were crying. I thought to myself: "This is not the argumentative scholar." I thought of stepping in and comforting you. Then I thought that all women must cry at some moments, everything can't always be perfect. I know you want to love. You need Amit—draw him closer. Don't take the vow that you'll never marry. I fear your obstinacy—once you've made up your mind, it's impossible to change it.'

Lavanya remained mute. With her head bowed, she kept pressing and folding the loose end of her sari in her lap. Yogamaya went on: 'Watching you, I see that so much learning has made you supple and subtle. The world you've created is not fit for people like us. You can't do without such mental illuminations, as though bodies of flesh and blood don't count. In our days, there was no such thing! Such illuminations didn't suffuse the joys and sorrows of life—not that there were no problems. They were plentiful. But nowadays, nothing is simple any longer.'

Lavanya smiled. Only the other day, Amit had been explaining to Yogamaya all about how the rays of illumination inform an argument. Yogamaya understood the subtlety of that; Yogamaya's mother, in her generation, couldn't have understood such an argument. Lavanya said, 'Mashima, the more clearly we grasp the working of the notion of time, the better able we are to resist its shock. We fear darkness, we cannot bear the agony of its sorrow as it remains obscure in our vision.'

'I now feel it would have been better had the two of you never met.'

'Please don't say that! I can't imagine anything else other than the fact that we have met. I used to think that books were all I had in my life. I now know I can love. That the impossible has become possible means a lot to me. I thought I was only a shadow, now I know I am real. What else can I expect? Just don't ask me to get married, please!'

Saying this, she slipped down from her chair, buried her head in Yogamaya's lap and began to weep.

9

Change of Residence

BACK HOME IN Calcutta, everyone was certain that Amit would be back from Shillong within a week or two. Naren Mitter had put out a bet that it wouldn't even be a week. But months passed, and there was no word from him. The lease on the house that Amit had rented from the Zamindar of Rangpur had expired. He came from Rangpur to occupy it. After a good deal of looking around, Amit found a cottage near Yogamaya's home. At one time, it had belonged to a milkman or a maintenance man. Then, it was rented to an office clerk, who touched it up a little. The clerk was dead—his widow put it up for rent. There were no windows. The three elements of heat, light and air could hardly penetrate it. On rainy days, the fourth element, water, poured in great profusion through its obscure holes.

Yogamaya was shocked when she visited one day. 'Why

are you putting yourself through this ordeal?' she exclaimed.

'Uma went without food for her penance. Mine consists of depriving myself of all creature comforts, giving up the couch, a desk and chair, till I'm close to these blank walls. Her penance was high up on the Himalayas, mine is amidst these hills of Shillong. There, a bride wished for a groom; here, a groom wishes to have a bride. There, Narada was the match-maker; here, Mashima is present. Now, if it should happen that the poet Kalidasa will not show up here, I shall necessarily do his work as best as I can.'

Amit laughed as he spoke, but his words pained Yogamaya. She almost invited him to move into her house, but restrained herself. 'In this drama of destiny, my intervention may complicate matters,' she thought. She sent a few things from her house, her pity for Amit redoubled. She kept telling Lavanya, 'Don't refuse to open up your heart to Amit.'

After a heavy shower one day, Yogamaya decided to visit Amit. She found him seated under a desk, reading a book in English. His room flooded, he had found shelter under the desk. He had a good laugh at himself, then he began his discourse on poetry. But his mind was distracted. He was thinking about Yogamaya's house, but he couldn't go there now. He had bought an expensive raincoat in Calcutta, where it was not needed. He had forgotten to bring it here, where it was sorely needed. He had an umbrella of sorts, but he had left it somewhere, probably under a deodar tree. Entering the room, Yogamaya exclaimed, 'What is the matter, Amit?'

Emerging from under the desk, Amit responded, 'My room today is in shambles, but its condition is a little better than mine!'

'It's not just in shambles, it is a disaster.'

'The roof of this room is like India. It is not a sum of its parts, it is listless. If there is a downpour, there is a riot of tears all over the place; if there is a gust of wind from outside, there rises a chorus of deep sighs inside. In protest, I've made some modifications over my head—it is under a platform. It is like the Home Rule in the midst of massive misgovernment. A fundamental principle of politics is evident here.'

'What fundamental principle?'

'The self-help improvised by a poor tenant is much more effective than the rule of an absentee landlord.'

Yogamaya was angry with Lavanya. Her growing affection for Amit became a flurry of superlatives. 'Such learning, such intellect, yet so unaffected and simple! How nice and charming are his words! What power of expression! As for looks, he seems better-looking than Lavanya. An unusual constellation of lucky stars has created a condition for Lavanya to have Amit so attracted to her. She is indeed lucky! Yet, Lavanya is hurting such a wonderful young man. For no rhyme or reason, she has declared she will not marry! As if she were an omnipotent, unreachable goddess. What insufferable vanity! The wretched girl is destined for a tragic end.'

For a moment, Yogamaya had thought of asking Lavanya to get into her car and go to Amit's house. On second thought, she had merely said, 'Just wait! I'll be back soon.'

On returning home, she found Lavanya reclining on a sofa, her feet tucked under a shawl. She was reading *Mother* by Maxim Gorky. She saw the sharp contrast. Seeing her so comfortable and cosy, Yogamaya became even angrier.

'Let us go out for a while,' she said to Lavanya.

'I don't feel like going out today, Mashima.'

Yogamaya didn't realize that Lavanya had turned to her book to escape from herself.

The whole afternoon, after lunch, she had waited restlessly for Amit to come. Every now and then, she would tell herself, 'Here he comes!' Outside, the pine trees swayed back and forth in the stormy wind, and torrents of rain fell impetuously. Lavanya felt an irrepressible urge to hold Amit's hands and say, 'I'm all yours!' The sky howled, the forests trembled, the hills were drenched in rain. Let Amit come and listen to Lavanya speak! Hours passed by. There was no sign of him. The long wait was painful. Lavanya walked to the porch and let the rains soak her. A deep sadness enveloped her mind, she was sunk in disappointment. She lost her inner strength to accept Amit as her own. She turned to her book.

That was the moment Yogamaya invited her to go out. She didn't feel like she had the energy. Pulling up a chair, Yogamaya sat in front of Lavanya. 'Do you love Amit?'

'Why do you ask?' Lavanya was surprised.

'If you don't love him, tell him the plain truth. If you don't want him, let him go.'

Lavanya's heart pounded. She couldn't speak.

'What I saw of him just now was enough to break my heart. Any girl loved by someone like Amit would consider herself extremely fortunate.'

Lavanya struggled to speak. At last, she said, 'You've asked me about love. I can't imagine anyone could love more than I do. I can die for it. My past is buried. I have a new beginning—a beginning without end. What has come over me?'

Yogamaya was stunned. She had always thought Lavanya was self-centred, content with herself. How could she have concealed this inner passion? Softly, gently, she said, 'Lavanya, my dear, don't suppress your feelings. Let them out. Amit is trying hard to reach out to you. Let him get to know you as you really are. Don't be afraid. Let Amit feel the fire inside you. Come, dear, come with me right now.' They set out for Amit's cottage.

10

The Next Phase

AMIT SPREAD SHEETS of newspaper on the wet chair and sat down at his desk. He was writing his autobiography. If asked what was in it, he would say that his life just revealed itself to him, like the hills of Shillong on a morning after rain. He had realized the meaning of his life at long last—how could he help revealing it? Usually, a man's biography is written after his death because others need to know who he was, so that he begins to live again in the minds of men. While in Shillong, one part of Amit died, then he began to live again like a resplendent light against the background of darkness. It was necessary to let the world know. Most lives drag on from birth to death in the shadow of twilight, like bats in a cave.

There was a mild drizzle outside. The storm had subsided and the clouds had cleared.

Amit got up from his chair and greeted Yogamaya.

'This is a surprise. I'm absolutely unprepared for it. What will Miss Lavanya think?'

'Let Miss Lavanya think a little. She needs to. Why should Mr Amit be so nervous?'

'Miss Lavanya should see Mr Amit at his best. The beggar's penury may be exposed to Mashima.'

'Why this discrimination, son?'

'In my own interest. One can claim riches by offering riches. Indigence can invite sympathy. The world owes its glory to its Miss Lavanyas and its humility to its Mahimas.'

'One can have both Lavanya and Mashima in one, Amit. It may not be necessary to hide one's indigence.'

'The answer may come only in the words of a poet. What I can say in prose will need commentary in verse. Matthew Arnold has called poetry the "criticism of life". I would put it differently; I would say "life's commentary is in verse". Let me caution my guests—what I'm about to recite is not by any poet laureate.'

Do not seek with empty hands,
What is sought with whole heart,
Nor with eyes wet standing at the door

'Just consider, love itself is fulfilment, its longings are not those of a pauper. When God loves his devotee, he comes to his door as a beggar.'

⟨❦⟩

In the abundance of giving
Garlands will be exchanged,
Will you place your goddess
On the pedestal of dust by the wayside

⟨❦⟩

'That's why I had said that I was unprepared for this surprise. Where can I offer a seat? On these wet newspapers? I fear the editor's rejection. The poet says, "I don't invite the object of my heart to share my thirst. I invite when my cup is full."'

⟨❦⟩

Among the blossoms of Spring
Shall I offer my blanket of love?
Let the lamps flare
Chase away darkness.

⟨❦⟩

'The first stage of life is infancy—the child is in Mashima's lap, his training is in tenderness. This cottage represents the same training. I have decided to name this cottage "Mashima's Bungalow".'

'The second stage of life, my son, is the glory of love. That is taking place in this cottage. No wet newspaper sheet can dampen that love. You're deluding yourself by thinking you've not found it. You know you have.'

Yogamaya asked Lavanya to stand next to Amit. She placed Lavanya's right hand on Amit's. She took Lavanya's gold necklace from her neck and tied their hands with it. 'Let the union of you two last forever,' she blessed.

Amit and Lavanya bent down to touch Yogamaya's feet. She said, 'Please wait for me here while I fetch some flowers from the garden.'

For a long time, the two remained silent. Then, raising her face to Amit's, Lavanya asked, 'Why didn't you come today?'

'I have no excuse. One has to draw up enough courage on a day like this to mention it. It is not written in the book of love that because of the want of a raincoat the man in love was unable to visit his beloved. The book says one must swim across the ocean if needed to reach his beloved. I'm swimming in the deep waters of the ocean of the heart. When shall I finish swimming?'

For we are bound where the mariner has not dared to go
And we will risk the ship, ourselves and all.

'Vanya, were you waiting for me today?'

'I was, Mita. The whole day, I was hoping to hear footfalls in the patter of rain. It seemed you were coming from afar. At long last, you've entered my life.'

'Vanya, there was all this time a void in my life, without you. Today, that void has filled. Light shines on it, the shadow of the whole sky covers it. It is beautiful. The fact that I'm talking away, speaking so many words, means that I'm overwhelmed with fulfilment.'

'Mita, how did you spend the whole day?'

'You were in my mind. I was about to say something to you. It was raining. I prayed: "Lend me the words, the words!"'

O, what is this?
Mysterious and uncapturable bliss
That I have known, yet seems to be
Simple as breath and easy as smile
And older than the earth

'I was borrowing another poet's verse, and making it mine. Had I the gift to set a tune, I would have sung from Vidyapati's song of rains, and made it my own.'

How shall I cry through
My nights and days without the Lord?

'How do I get by without the one who is the life of my life? Where shall I get the right tune for these

Amit and Lavanya

words? I raise my eyes and pray, now for words, now for music. With words and music to a different person—perhaps to your favourite poet Tagore.'

Lavanya laughed. 'Even those who love Tagore do not mention his name as often as you do!'

'Vanya, I'm talking too much. The monsoon has burst open the floodgates of garrulity in me. If you follow the weather report, you'll be staggered by the vagaries of my eccentricity. If I were in Calcutta, I would have taken you in a car and raced straight to Moradabad. I couldn't explain why. When a flood comes, it roars and races and sweeps time along, like foam, with its laughter.'

At this moment, Yogamaya returned with a bouquet full of sunflowers. 'Lavanya dear, touch Amit's feet with these flowers.' It was only a formality to show what was in Lavanya's heart.

Amit whispered into Lavanya's ears, 'Vanya, I must get a ring for you.'

'Why, Mita? Is it necessary?'

'By placing your hand in mine, you've given me more than I can dream of. Poets sing praises of the face of the beloved, but the hand is the signal of the heart. It captures the inexpressible language of love. This ring will wrap itself around your finger like a tiny word of my love. Just this. Mine! Let this little word ever cling to your hand, inscribed in gold.'

'Very well, as you wish.'

'I'll send for it from Calcutta. What is your favourite stone?'

'No stone. A pearl will do.'

'Excellent! I too love pearls.'

11

Discourse on Conjugal Union

IT WAS SETTLED that the wedding would take place in November. Yogamaya would go to Calcutta to make the necessary arrangements.

Lavanya told Amit, 'You were due back in Calcutta long ago. You were caught up in uncertainty all these days. Now that predicament is past. You may go back without any worry. We will meet again at the wedding.'

'Why this severe punishment?'

'The other day you talked about how happiness should be simple. Well, for the sake of preserving that simplicity.'

'These are wise words. I thought you were a poet the other day. Now I believe you're a philosopher. You have said it all: one has to be rigorous to make things simple. If you wish for a simple rhythm, it has to have pauses in the right places. It has to have restraint. All right. I'll leave tomorrow, remove myself from these joyful days. It's like that verse in the *Meghnadvadh Kavya*—those startling lines about bidding farewell: When he went to the land of death/Before it was time. I may leave Shillong, but the month of November will not run away from the calendar. Guess what I shall do in Calcutta?'

'What?'

'While Mashima will be busy making arrangements for the wedding day, I shall busy myself for the days after. People forget that living together as a married couple is an art; it has to be reinvented every day. Do you remember how King Aja had described Indumati in *Raghuvamsa?*'

Lavanya recalled: 'The dearest follower in every loving art.'

'This loving art is the core principle of wedded life. The ignorant think of wedding as a union—the real union of the hearts of the couple is ignored after the wedding.'

'Explain to me your conception of the art of union. If you wish to have me as your follower, let the lesson begin today.'

'Very well. The poet creates rhythm with voluntary restraint. Union must also be based on voluntary restraint. To take it for granted is self-deception. The joy of paying a heavy price is great indeed.'

'Let us hear how you come to estimate the right price.'

'Wait a bit. Let me first tell you what I've pictured in my mind, It is the bank of the Ganga near Diamond Harbour. A small steam launch carries one to Calcutta in a couple of hours.'

'How does Calcutta come in?'

'Calcutta plays no significant role in my life now, you

know that. I go to the library at the Bar not for work but to play chess. The other lawyers have realized that I'm not interested in practising law. My heart is not in it. They pass on a brief to me when the case can be amicably settled. It is not earning a living—it is for the sake of life. At the core of a mango, there is a hard shell. It is not sweet, nor soft, and you do not eat it. Yet, this shell, hard as it is, is the core of the mango, the basis of its form. The hardness of Calcutta is necessary, the hard core of Calcutta makes living there pleasurable.'

'I understand. This makes it equally necessary for me too. Shall I also go to Calcutta from 10 a.m. to 5 p.m.? Must I?'

'Not for the city but to go to work.'

'What sort of work? Work without pay?'

'Certainly not. You can teach in a women's college.'

'Very well. I like the idea. What else?'

'I can see it clearly. The bank of the Ganga. From its lowest slope rises a very old banyan tree, its many roots descending from its branches. When the trader Dhanapati was sailing down the Ganga to Sri Lanka, perhaps he had anchored his boat at this banyan tree, had his boat tied to this banyan tree, had cooked his food under its shade. To its right is the paved ghat overlaid with moss and with cracks all over. At the ghat, our slender boat, green and white, is anchored as well. On its blue banner, the name is printed in white. You better give it a name.'

'Shall I? Mitali.'

'Just the right name—Mitali. I had thought of calling it Sagari and felt good about the name. But I yield to your choice. It is better. A tiny stream runs through the garden. Over on that side is your house, on this mine.'

'Will you have to swim across every day? Do I have to keep a light on at my window?'

'We'll swim in our imagination while crossing the pole-bridge. The name of your house is Manasi. Now you have to give a name to mine.'

'Dipak.'

'A very good choice! I shall put a lamp befitting the name Dipak on the crest of my house. On the evening we have our union, a red light will glow there; on the night of separation, a blue one. On my return from Calcutta, I shall expect a letter from you every day. It may turn up, it may not. If I don't have it by eight in the evening, I shall curse my luck and try to read Bertrand Russell's *Book on Logic*. We'll have one fixed rule—I can't visit your house uninvited.'

'And I yours?'

'It will be good to follow the same rule. But on occasion, exceptions will be welcome.'

'And what if the breach itself becomes the rule—what a mess will that create in your house! Just think of it. I had better come wearing a burqa.'

'As you wish. But I'll need a letter of invitation. The letter needn't have anything except a line or two from a poem.'

'Will there be an invitation for me? Shall I be cast out?'

'You'll be invited once a month, on the full-moon night.'

'Now give me a sample of a letter to your favourite follower.'

'Very well.'

Taking his notebook from his pocket, Amit tore out a page and wrote on it:

⟡

How gently over my garden
Wind of the southern sea
In the hour my love cometh
And calleth me.

⟡

Lavanya kept the page. Amit said, 'Now you give me a sample.' Lavanya was about to write it on a scrap of paper. Amit protested: 'No, you must write it in my notebook.'

Lavanya wrote in Sanskrit, quoting the poet Jayadeva: Mita, thou art my life, my ornament thou./ The pearl of my life's ocean thou.

Putting the notebook back in his pocket, Amit remarked, 'It is interesting that I should have a woman's words, and you a man's. Nothing wrong with that. The flame looks the same, whether the burning log is from the simul tree or the bokul.'

Lavanya said, 'We've exchanged the invitation. What next?'

Amit replied, 'The evening star shines, the Ganga swells with the tidal waves, the wind sings in rows of casuarinas, the waters lap on the knotted roots of the banyan tree. In your backyard is a lotus pond, you've bathed at its solitary ghat, you've combed your hair. You change the colours of your saris from day to day. I wonder what colour it would be this evening. The place we meet is not fixed. Some days, we meet on the platform beneath the champak tree; on others, at the terrace on the bank of the river. I've bathed in the Ganga, I am wearing a white muslin dhoti, a chaddar and a pair of wooden sandals inlaid with ivory. When I arrive, I see you seated on a carpet, a garland of flowers on a silver platter in front of you, sandalwood paste in a tiny bowl and incense burning in a corner. We'll travel for a couple of months during the autumn holidays, but to different places. If you go to the hills, I'll go to a seaside resort. These are my proposed routines of our marriage. What do you think?'

'I like them.'

'Just like?'

'What you need to do, I'll accept, even though I may not need to do the same.'

'That's not fair.'

'However near you may be, you're still far. It's not necessary to have rules to maintain that distance. There's nothing in me that can escape your scrutiny. That's why it makes sense to live in separate quarters on the two sides of the river.'

Amit sprang up from his chair and said, 'I hear you! Forget the garden. We'll not move out of Calcutta. I'll rent an apartment above Niranjan's office, where both of us shall live. There is nothing like near and far in our world. On the left side of a five-foot bedstead will be where you will sleep, it will be your Manasi; on the right, I'll be at Dipak. On the east side of the room, there will be a dresser with a mirror; on the west, a bookcase that will shield us from the sun. The books will be meant for two readers only. North of the room, there will be a sofa, again for the two of us to sit on. A few paces away, just behind the clothes rack, you'll stand. With my nervous hands, I'll hold out a letter of invitation.'

Gently blows over the terrace
Wind of the South sweet,
With my beloved on my side
Our eyes will meet.

'Does it sound bad, Vanya?'

'Not at all, Mita. But where did you get it?'

'From my friend Nilmadhav. He was looking for a wife. But inspired by the hopes of finding one, he translated the English poem in his typical Calcutta fashion. With an MA in economics, he then got married, with a big dowry in cash, gold jewellery. The four eyes and the South sweet met. He had no use for the poem any more. He didn't mind giving it away.'

'The southern breeze will blow over your terrace too, but will your new bride remain new forever?'

Thumping the desk, Amit shouted, 'She will! She will! She will remain new forever!'

Yogamaya walked in from the next room and asked, 'What will remain, Amit? Not the desk, obviously!'

'Whatever deserves to endure will survive in this world. Finding a new bride is a stroke of luck. Once you find one, she'll remain a bride forever.'

'Let us have an example.'

'The day I have one, I'll show you.'

'It seems it will be a while. In the meantime, come and have lunch.'

12

The Last Evening

AFTER FINISHING LUNCH, Amit told Yogamaya, 'I'm leaving for Calcutta tomorrow, Mashima. My relatives suspect I've turned into a tribal!'

'Do your relatives know that you change easily?'

'Only too well. Why else would they be relatives? That doesn't prove I'm a quick-change artist or capable of turning into a tribal. The change I've gone through is actually a transformation. I am in love. Mashima, please allow me to take Lavanya out today. Together, we will say farewell to the hills of Shillong.'

Yogamaya gave her permission.

Amit and Lavanya walked holding hands, their bodies close together. The solitary path they took led to a thick forest. It had a bare spot with open skies, where one could watch the sunset. The two of them stood there. Amit drew Lavanya's face close to his. Her eyes were half-closed, tears trickled down her face. The golden sky was breaking into colours of ruby and emerald; through the gaps in the thinning clouds, one could see the limpid blue sky, intense, blissful and musical. Slowly it grew dark. In the descending gloom, the little patch of open sky seemed like a flower, its petals closing.

'Let us go back,' whispered Lavanya. She wanted the beautiful moment to end. Amit grasped Lavanya in a warm embrace.

'I'll have to leave early in the morning,' Amit said, 'I'll not see you before I go.'

'Why not?'

'The Shillong chapter of our encounter should fittingly end today, at this lovely spot. Here ends the first canto, our prelude to paradise.'

Lavanya said nothing. She walked on, Amit's hand in hers. In her heart, she felt happiness mingled with streaks of sadness. She had never thought she would feel such unimaginable intimacy. She wanted to bend down to touch Amit's feet and say: 'You've truly made me blessed'—but the words remained unspoken.

As they approached the house, Amit said, 'Vanya, speak your last words, bidding me farewell in verse so that I can remember it. Some little thing, whatever comes to your mind.'

Lavanya thought for a moment, then recited:

❧

I brought you no happiness, only the gift of freedom,
At this luminous end of night.
No prayers, no importunity
No piles of abjectness
No vanity, no piteous tears
No proud laughter
No turning back,
Only the offering of freedom
I've filled in the basket
As I reach my dreadful end.

❧

'Very unfair of you, Vanya. This is not what you should say on a day like this—never! What prompted you to think of this? Please take it back—at once!'

'What are you afraid of, Mita? This love, tested by fire, makes no claim to happiness. It is free itself, that is why it can confer freedom. It brings in its train no weariness, no sadness. What can be a better gift?'

'Where did you get this from? I want to know.'

'Rabindranath Tagore.'

'I never saw it in any of his books.'

'It has not yet been published in a book.'

'How did you get hold of it then?'

'My father had a student who was deeply devoted to him. My father bestowed on him knowledge from intellect. But there was hunger in his heart, which drove him whenever he had time to read Tagore, to gather from him gems of poems.'

'And he brought and offered them to you?'

'He lacked that courage. He would just leave it somewhere where it might catch my eye or fall into my hand.'

'Were you kind to him?'

'I didn't have the chance. I pray that fate be kind to him.'

'I can see that the poem you've recited is the voice of that unfortunate heart.'

'Indeed, it was.'

'What made you think of it today?'

'How can I say? There was another piece too, which also came to my mind today—I don't know why.'

O the lovely! You've filled your eyes with tears
You've kindled in my heart the fire of the unbearable,
In that fire sorrow is tempered
And there infatuation ends
The petals of the lotus
Of separation
Blossom in its warmth.

'Vanya, why has this man come between us today? I'm not jealous, I hate jealousy. However, a fear grips my mind. Tell me what made you recall, today of all days, the poems he left?'

'A day after he left for good, I found these on the desk

he used for his studies. Besides these, there were bunches of other poems by Rabindranath, almost a bookful. These were farewell poems. Today, I'm bidding you farewell.'

'Can that farewell compare with this?'

'How can I say? Why argue about them? I like these poems. That is why I recited them to you. No other reason.'

'Vanya, until people completely forget Rabindranath's poems, his good works will not come into their own. That is why I don't use him. Popular appreciation is like the mist that doesn't lift to clear the sky.'

'Look, Mita, what a woman likes she keeps to herself, doesn't discuss it with others. She pays all she can, she doesn't care to bargain for it.'

'Then I have hope. I shall conceal the market value of my work and wait for the seal of your approval.'

'We are near our house. Let me hear your farewell poem.'

'Don't be upset, Vanya. I'll not be able to recite from Tagore.'

'Why should I be upset?'

'I have a special poet whose style I like.'

'I've been hearing about him from you ever since we met. I've written to Calcutta for his books.'

'Good heavens! His books! The fellow has many shortcomings, but sending his works to a publisher is not one of them. You'll get to know him through me, otherwise . . .'

'Don't worry, Mita. I'm confident I'll appreciate him as you do.'

'How so?'

'What I like is mine, what you like will be mine too. This is where our two minds will meet. Our bookshelf in Calcutta will have enough room to hold both our choices. Now, out with your poem.'

'I don't feel like reciting it now. I'm distracted by our arguments.'

'Forget the arguments. Please go ahead.'

Amit straightened his hair and began:

O beautiful! You're the early morning star
Shining over the crest of mountains
With the night over
You're still visible in the distant horizon.

'You see, Vanya, it's the moon asking the evening star to keep it company through the night. It is no longer in love with the night.'

Where the earth meets the sky
I'm the half-awake half moon,
A dim light
In darkness.

'This half-wakefulness and partial luminosity expresses its sorrow. It tries to pierce the veil of triviality, struggles through its sleep all night. What a grand idea!'

⁓⁓

My seat is spread
In the great void of sleep
I string with finger as I dream.
Ruffling lightly the trance.

⁓⁓

'The burden of such a slight existence is heavy indeed. The dying river collects dirt in its sluggish flow.'

⁓⁓

With slow steps I move
To the end of my journey.
My music fails
I'm down and weary.

⁓⁓

'This weariness is not its end. It has hopes of turning the loose strings of the veena, somewhere beyond the horizon one hears some footsteps.'

Come, O lovely early morning star
Before the night runs its course.
What I missed in my dream
Let me have it as I wake.

'There is hope of redemption. One can hear the great cacophony of a waking world. Lamp in hand, the harbinger of the great path is about to arrive.'

Lift it from the abyss of night
Render it to morn,
What was lost in darkness
Bring it out to light.
The silence of sleep ends
In the nightly rhythm of the heavens
There let me proffer my veena,
I, the half-awake moon.

'I am this miserable moon. I'll be off early morning tomorrow. I wish to fill the void of departure with the song of awakening of the early morning star. What obscure dream shall reveal itself in full glory in the light of the early morning star? There is in this poem the anticipation of hope, the luminosity of dawn, unlike the hopelessness and despair in Tagore.'

'Why are you so angry with Tagore and bring him up time and again to castigate him?'

'You've all made too much of him!'

'Don't say that, Mita. What I like is my own. It's not my fault if it is disagreeable to others or to you. Let me give you my word—I'll listen to your poet, but I'll not impose mine on you when we move to the apartment in Calcutta.'

'That's not fair. Marriage means accommodating each other's interests.'

'You'll never allow those you don't like to your literary world; I, on the other hand, will welcome all.'

'This argument has not been good. It has spoilt our last evening together.'

'Not in the least. Plain-speaking will enrich our life.'

'I must get rid of this bad taste in my mouth. Bengali verse won't do. English poetry cools my temper. On my return to India, I was a professor for a while.'

Lavanya laughed. 'Our temper is like the bulldog in an English home. It growls at the sight of a dhoti. But the sight of liveried servants sets its tail wagging.'

'I agree. Being partial to something is not material and spontaneous. It is, in most cases, made to order. To be partial to English literature has been instilled in us from childhood. We're afraid to be critical of English literature, while we do not appreciate our own. Anyway, today, no Nivaran Chakravarti but pure English—no translating.'

'No, Mita. Let us wait until we settle in our apartment

for English poetry. Now, for our last sunset together, let us have Nivaran Chakravarti. No one else!'

'Long live Nivaran!' Amit exclaimed exultantly. 'He has attained full recognition in your mind, Vanya. I shall appoint him your poet laureate. He'll accept no laurels from other hands.'

'Will that please him?'

'If it doesn't, I'll throw him out!'

'Fine, that may happen later. Right now, let me hear you recite.'

Amit began.

~~~

Patiently, you stayed by me,
Days and nights on end!
How often I heard your footfall
On the path of my destiny!
Now that I'm about to leave
Let me offer you a parting gift
A hymn of celebration.
How often I laboured in vain,
My sacred fire wouldn't break into flames,
Only despairs of smoke rose in it.
How often the evanescent flame
Painted its faint signs
On the insentient night,
Before it vanished in the void.
Now, the sacred fire
Burns fervently at your advent.
What was futile will now be fulfilled.

I dedicate to you
My offering of the day,
My homage,
Let your tender touch
Bless my bowed head,
Wherever you reign in glory
Let my hymn and respect
Find their place.

13

Misgivings

IT WAS DIFFICULT for Lavanya to turn to her work this morning. She didn't go out for her stroll. Amit had said he didn't want to see her in the morning before he left Shillong. She deferred to Amit's wishes and restrained herself. Yogamaya was used to taking a shower early in the morning, then going out to pick some flowers to offer to the gods. Today, Lavanya got up before Yogamaya and came to the foot of the eucalyptus. She held a couple of books in her hands, perhaps to fool herself, or perhaps others, that she was reading seriously. The books lay open, time passed, not a page was turned. Her great day had been yesterday, she assured herself. The morning sky was all light and shade. Amit, she was convinced, was an escapist. Once he slipped away, he would never return. He would start talking seriously one day, and the next day, forget what he had said the day before. Lavanya thought that Amit would forget all the wonderful things he had said yesterday. A sense of dissatisfaction descended on her, reflected in the poignancy of the morning light.

Around nine in the morning, Amit turned up, shouting at the top of his voice: 'Mashima, Mashima!'

Yogamaya was in the kitchen. She had been thinking about how much she would miss Amit when he was gone. She hadn't asked Lavanya to help with the household chores, assuming she wanted to be left alone.

Lavanya was startled. The book fell from her lap.

Yogamaya stepped out of the kitchen and said, 'What is the matter, Amit? Why, is there an earthquake?'

'Yes, an earthquake. I was ready to leave, went to the post office to check if I had any mail. I got this telegram.'

'I hope all is well,' Yogamaya said. Lavanya came into the room.

Amit replied, 'My sister Cissie, her friend Katie Mitter and her brother Naren are due to arrive this evening.'

'What is there to worry about? I gather that the house near the racetrack is vacant. If that is not available, we can make room in our house.'

'That is not what worries me, Mashima. As a matter of fact, they have booked rooms in a hotel in Shillong.'

'I'll not let your sister see you living in that shack. She might think we're responsible.'

'No, Mashima, my paradise is lost. Farewell to my shack! I'll have to stay with them in the hotel.'

Lavanya's face fell. She had never thought of the social distance that separated Amit's family and hers. The fact that Amit was leaving for Calcutta was not a concern, but the fact that he had to move to a fancy hotel had her worried. Perhaps their dream house on the bank of the river would never materialize.

'I may have to go to a hotel or to hell,' Amit said to Yogamaya, casting a sidelong glance at Lavanya. 'My real home is here!'

Amit had hoped that his sisters and their friends would not descend on him in Shillong. He had been receiving his mail at Yogamaya's address. He hadn't thought that that would cause any problems. His anxiety now showed.

It was difficult for Yogamaya to understand why the arrival of his sister would be a matter of concern. Lavanya thought Amit was uncomfortable about being seen in her company in front of his sister.

Amit turned to Lavanya. 'Do you have a moment? Could we go for a walk?'

Lavanya replied, 'No, I have work to do.'

'Do go out for a bit, dear,' Yogamaya encouraged Lavanya.

'Mashima,' Lavanya replied, 'Surama's studies have been neglected. I am to blame. From now on, there will be no excuses.'

Yogamaya knew the obstinate streak in Lavanya. She did not insist any further.

'I must be off,' said Amit. 'I must have everything ready for them.'

But before he left, he stood still for a while on the porch. 'Vanya,' he said, 'you can see the roof of my house through the trees. I didn't tell you—I've bought the house. The owner was surprised. She probably thought I had found a stash of gold in the shack. She increased the price. I found gold there all right, but only I knew it. My glorious shack will be mine alone.'

Lavanya looked grim. She said, 'Why do you worry? Let everyone know! The truth should come out, then no one would complain.'

Amit replied, 'Vanya, after our wedding, we must come and stay here in the cottage. The dream house on the banks of the Ganga by the banyan tree is here. The name you picked—"Mitali"—suits it perfectly.'

'When you next want to enter it, you'll find it inadequate, too small for you. In today's world, there is no room for tomorrow. The other day, you said that man's first initiation is in embracing voluntary poverty. The second is in accumulating wealth. The final stage is the renunciation of the world.'

'Vanya, that is what Tagore says. He says that Shahjahan has transcended even his Taj Mahal. It didn't occur to him that we only build in order to transcend what we've built. In the world of creativity, that is evolution. Something happens, and the demons within us dictate "Create!" Once you've created it, there is no longer a need for the thing that was created. But that doesn't mean that giving up is the ultimate thing. Shahjahans and Mumtazes celebrated immortality. That is why the Taj has never been rendered futile. Nivaran Chakravarti has composed a poem, a rejoinder to your poet's ode to the Taj Mahal. He wrote it on a postcard.'

~~~~~

You'll be left alone
When the night is startled
At the onset of dawn,
Alas, O Bridal Chamber
Separation lurks in the horizon,
It tears the garland to pieces
The one exchanged by the two lovers.
You are everlasting,
Your festival celebration
Is without end.
Who says the lovers ever
Return at your call,
At your threshold.
Love knows no death,
You too are immortal.

~~~~~

'Tagore always harps on the things that pass away. He doesn't celebrate the abiding. Vanya, does the poet say that when the two of us knock at the door, it will not let us in?'

'I beg you, Mita, please don't start a fight between poets. Don't you think I didn't know from the very first that you are the Nivaran Chakravarti that you speak of? Don't start building a memorial to our love in verse. At least wait until it dies.'

Lavanya understood that, by talking relentlessly, Amit was suppressing an inner anxiety. Amit too realized that the poetic battle of the previous evening had not been inharmonious. But this morning, it sounded out of place. That Lavanya had seen through it made him feel awkward. He said, 'All right, I'm off. I too have things to do. At this moment, I have to check out the hotel. It seems that poor Nivaran's tenure as a poet is over.'

Lavanya grasped Amit's hand and said, 'Please, Mita, bear with me and forgive me. When the day comes for parting, I beg you not to leave me with anger in your heart.'

She hurriedly went inside to control her tears.

Amit stood there. Then slowly, almost absent-mindedly, he went towards the eucalyptus tree. He saw the broken walnut shells. The sight saddened him. He then noticed a book lying on the grass. It was Tagore's *Balaka*. The last page of the book was wet. He thought he would go in and return the book; instead, he put it in his pocket. He thought of going to the hotel; instead, he sat under the tree. The clouds of the night had washed the sky clear. The dusty air had settled. The distant hills and forests seemed starkly etched out against the blue sky. The world seemed close and intimate. Time passed.

Lavanya wanted to turn to work. She saw Amit seated under the tree. She couldn't wait. With tears in her eyes, she went up to him and asked, 'Mita, what are you thinking of?'

'The opposite of what I have always thought of till now.'

'You are never happy until you have turned your mind upside down. Well, tell me what is on your mind now.'

'All along, I was building a dream home with you in it. Sometimes, it was by the Ganga; sometimes, in the hills. Today, the vision of a path running up the hill, shaded with rows of trees stirs in my mind. I'm holding an iron rod, a square haversack with leather straps on my shoulder. You are walking beside me. Vanya, you have swept me out of the house and set me on this path. The house is full of people. However, this path is for us two alone.'

'So the garden near Diamond Harbour is gone. The apartment in the city is gone too. Very well. How would you keep us separate? At the end of the day, you'll spend the night in one rest house and I in another?'

'No need, Vanya. Moving constantly keeps one young forever. There is no time to get old. Age comes with immobility.'

'Why this sudden change of mind, Mita?'

'I shall tell you. I've had an unexpected mail from Shobhanlal. You may have heard of him—the reputed award-winning scholar. He has set out on a tour to retrace the ancient routes of Indian history. He wants to recover the past. I want to chart the new paths of the future.

'At one time, he was obsessed with the idea of rediscovering the ancient route through Kapish in Afghanistan. Xuan Zhang had come to India as a pilgrim by that road, and before that, Alexander with his army. Shobhanlal learnt Pashtu along with the laws and customs of the Pathans. He is a handsome fellow; in his loose outfit, he looks like an Iranian. He asked me to give him letters of introduction to some French scholars who are doing similar research in that country. I studied with them when I was in France. I gave him the letters, but the Indian government refused to give him a passport. Since then, he has been looking for those ancient routes, in Kashmir, in the Kumaon hills. Now, he wants to explore the eastern end of the Himalayas to locate the routes through which the Buddhist missions had passed. His wanderlust makes me restless too. We wear our eyes out looking for the routes of the world in books, while this maniac is out to read the book of the road itself, written by the hand of destiny. Do you know what I think?'

'What?'

'I think he was disappointed in love in his youth, which explains his wanderlust. I don't know the whole story, but one day, when we were alone, we talked through the night. The moon rose in view through the blooming jarul tree. He told me about someone, he never mentioned the name. No sooner had he started talking about her than he was choked with emotion and hurried away. Somewhere in his life, he was cruelly wounded. He is trying to overcome that pain by ceaseless travel.'

Lavanya, all of a sudden, grew deeply interested in botany. She bent down to examine a white-and-yellow wildflower in the grass and began to count its petals.

'Vanya,' Amit went on, 'you've pushed me out on the road today.'

'How?'

'I built the house in my mind. This morning it seemed that you were reluctant to move into it. For over two months, I have been preparing it. I called you today:

"Come, my bride, into this house!" But you cast away the veil and said, "There is no room here, beloved. Our seven-step wedding will be an endless march.'"

Lavanya's botanical focus broke. She stood up suddenly and, with a lump in her throat, said, 'Please, Mita, no more! I have no time.'

14

The Comet

AMIT REALIZED THAT every Bengali in Shillong knew of his relationship with Lavanya. The main topic of gossip among clerks in the government office was who ruled the planets in the secretarial heaven. They noticed a pair of stars in the solar system. Like good observers of celestial bodies, they naturally began to discuss the ways in which the fiery drama of these new luminaries began.

Among the gossipers was Kumar Mukherjee, an attorney. Some called him Kumar Mukho, while others Mr Mukho. Lissie's circle of friends knew him, although he wasn't part of the core group. Amit liked to call him the Comet. The reason was that even though he was outside their set, he wagged his way into their orbit. Everyone knew he was attracted to Lissie. She, however, was angry and upset about this.

Amit ran into Kumar in Shillong every now and then.

It was hard not to notice him. He had never been to England; nevertheless, he did not fail to flash his English manners. A long, fat cigar was always at his mouth, justifying his nickname, Mukho the comet. Amit tried to avoid him and believed that the Comet was unaware of it. To see and yet not see is a subtle art.

Kumar had put together a dossier from the local Bengalis, which we may label 'Amit Ray Runs Riot'. The greatest scandalmongers are the greatest lovers of scandal. Kumar had come to Shillong for health reasons. But the urge to spread gossip took him back to Calcutta within five days. There, in the presence of Cissie, Lissie and company, he told tales of Amit, his descriptions farcical and droll.

Cissie's object of attention was Naren, Katie Mitter's elder brother. The rumour was that they were soon to be joined in matrimony. Cissie was willing, but pretended not to be. Naren had hoped that Amit would help him in his quest for Cissie's hand, but he proved unreachable at this point. He wouldn't return to Calcutta, nor would he answer his letters. Naren had hurled all the abusive, vicious words that he knew in English, in public and in private, at Amit. He had even sent him telegrams in Shillong, but to no avail. At long last, it was decided that the matter needed investigation at the spot. In this matter, even more enthusiastic than Cissie was Katie Mitter.

Naren had lived in Europe for a long time. The son of a rich zamindar, he had no need to earn a living or worry about being a spendthrift. He had no interest in learning. His main concern was expending both money and time.

He styled himself an artist. He had lived in many bohemian parts of Europe. He gave up painting after his well-wishers frankly advised him to turn to something else. He now pretended to be an art critic. If he couldn't be a good painter, at least he could critique what was not good art. He turned his moustache upwards in the French fashion; he was just as careful about keeping his hair unkempt. He was good-looking enough, but in order to make himself look more attractive, he had stashed his dresser with all sorts of French beauty aids. He would throw away a Havana cigar after a few puffs. He sent his clothes to be laundered in Paris every month by post. His sartorial measurements were entered in the premier tailoring houses of Europe, where the royals of Patiala and Kapurthala sent for their clothing. He accented his English with a sluggish drawl. Many in the know testified that he spoke like blue-blooded English aristocrats. He had an enviable command of slang, which many in his circle of friends admired.

Katie Mitter's real name was Ketaki. Her manners were patterned on her brother's—they were both very chic and very English. She condescendingly rejected the average Bengali woman's long hair and applied the scissors to her own with a measure of pride; her hair, like the tail of a tadpole, had transformed itself into the bob of a fashionable model. She coated her naturally fair complexion with enamel. In her childhood, Katie's dark eyes had been gentle and serene; now, they were arrogant and withdrawn. They glittered like a half-drawn knife. Her lips, once sweet and unaffected, were set by constant sneering in the hard curve of a twisted goad. I am not an expert in women's wear. But what was striking about her attire was its extremely fine texture, delicate as the slough of a snake, through which one could glimpse the tint of her underwear. Her blouse exposed rather than covered her bust; her bare arms would rest now on a table, now on the arm of a chair. When she puffed a cigarette held between her manicured fingers, it was less for the sake of smoking than for its decorative effect. Her shoes were high-heeled and sharply pointed. The Creator had failed to fashion the human foot in the model of a goat's hoof; this was now corrected by torturing the earth with the elevated tread of this issue of the cobbler's art.

Cissie was still at the middle stage. She hadn't received her final degree yet, but she was getting promotions. She bubbled with laughter and charmed her admirers with her irrepressible chatter. She was womanly and demure one moment, girlish and immature the other. Her high heels were de rigueur, but older style showed in her unshorn chignon; while the lower end of her sari fell a few inches too high, its upper portion was still draped with modesty. She carried gloves unnecessarily, but still had bangles on both her wrists. She smoked with confidence, but was still tempted to chew paan every now and then. She did not mind having pickles and preserves in a tin meant for biscuits; between the plum pudding at Christmas and the Bengali rice cakes in winter, she really preferred the latter. She learned ballroom dancing by taking lessons from an English teacher, but felt rather shy about dancing in another man's arms on a public floor.

They all hurried to Shillong, upset by stories churned out on the rumour mill. Lavanya was classed as a 'governess'. They had no doubt that she had attached herself to Amit to seek wealth and fortune. They had to rescue him from her clutches. The four-headed Brahma ogles women with four pairs of eyes—no wonder he has made man dull-witted where woman is concerned! They had to gather in Shillong to get Amit out of this mess.

The two women arrived at an understanding between themselves as to the general plan of action. It was out of the question to let Amit know anything about their plans. In the meantime, they would be prepared to do battle.

The first thing they noticed about Amit was that he had acquired a rustic look. Amit, of course, was never like the rest of his social set. He was urbane and fastidious. A tanned and a rustic touch had settled on him. To them, he looked foolish. He behaved like an ordinary person. His favourite sport had been to poke fun at everything. Now, he would have none of that.

Cissie told him bluntly, 'Before we came, we thought you'd turned tribal. You've actually become green like the pine trees around here. Your health may have improved, but you're no longer interesting.'

Amit quoted Wordsworth on what Nature does to one's body and mind—the spirit of 'mute insensate things'.

Cissie said to herself, 'We have no quarrel with the mute insensate things. What we are afraid of are not mute, they are sweet-tongued talkers.'

They had expected Amit to mention Lavanya. Days passed by, and Amit said not a word. One thing was obvious: Amit's heart was not there with them. Long before they got up in the morning, Amit would be gone somewhere, and when he returned, he would have a drooping expression on his face. Even more alarming was that he had a book by Tagore on his bed. On the inside cover was Lavanya's name, with the first two letters crossed out with red ink.

Every now and then, Amit would disappear. He was working to grow his appetite, he would say. That the appetite was strong was obvious to all. But they pretended they didn't know. Cissie laughed, Katie burnt with jealousy. Amit was so absorbed in his own problems that he didn't notice that the others were alarmed. He would tell the two women he had gone to look for a waterfall; it never occurred to him that the others would wonder what kind of waterfall it had been, whether it had any water in it.

This morning, he announced he was going to look for orange honey. When the two women showed interest in joining him, Amit replied that the road was rough and inaccessible by any means of transportation. He left before the discussion could reach an end. The two friends decided to delay no longer and launched their expedition to that orange honey orchard. Naren had gone to the races. He had wanted to take Cissie with him, but Cissie had declined.

15

Interruption

THE TWO WOMEN entered Yogamaya's garden, but couldn't find anyone. They saw on the terrace a teacher with her pupil, engaged in giving lessons. It was easy to guess the teacher was Lavanya. Walking up the steps, Katie said in English, 'Sorry.' Lavanya got up and asked, 'What do you want, please?' Katie looked at Lavanya and asked sharply, 'We came to find whether Mr Amit Raiye is here.' Lavanya couldn't follow her accent, and wondered who that could be. So she said, 'We don't know him.'

The two friends exchanged sneering glances. Katie hissed, 'We know he comes here oftener than is good for him.' Lavanya was startled—she realized who they were. 'Let me call Mashima.' She was embarrassed. 'She'll tell you everything.'

Once Lavanya had gone inside the house, Katie turned to Surama and asked, 'Is she your teacher?'

'Yes.'

'Lavanya by name, I believe?'

'Yes.'

'Got matches?' asked Katie in English. Confused by the sudden question, Surama failed to grasp what was being said. She stared at Katie.

'Matches,' explained Katie in Bengali. Surama fetched a box. Lighting a cigarette, Katie asked, 'Learning English?'

Surama nodded, then ran inside the house.

'The girl may or may not have learnt much from her governess, but certainly not manners. The famous Lavanya! Delicious! They have turned the Shillong hills into a volcano. What tremors of an earthquake have shaken Amit's heart. Silly! Men are funny.'

Cissie laughed out loud. She didn't dislike men for their follies. Why, she herself had caused a few earthquakes in men's hearts, but this was the limit. On the one hand, there was a woman like Katie; on the other, the governess who looked as though butter wouldn't melt in her mouth. What a bundle of wet rags! How could Amit have ever put up with her?

'Cissie, your brother's mind always hops on its head. In perverse ways, his contrary mind thinks of this woman as an angel.'

Katie put her cigarette on the Algebra book on the desk, opened her silver-chained vanity, powdered her face and re-pencilled her eyebrows. Cissie felt no resentment towards her brother for his choice, quite the contrary—

she was touched by it. She was angered by the false angels that men fall for. Katie had no patience with Cissie's amused indifference to her brother. She felt like shaking her.

At this moment, Yogamaya appeared, dressed in a white silk sari. Lavanya didn't come. Katie had brought along her poodle Tabby. He had been content with sniffing at Lavanya and Surama. But the sight of Yogamaya excited him. He rushed to her, and with his forepaws soiled Yogamaya's clean white sari. Cissie got hold of him by the collar. Katie tapped his nose with her forefinger. 'Naughty dog!' she scolded.

Katie didn't rise from her seat. She puffed at her cigarette and, turning her head, examined Yogamaya. She was angrier at Yogamaya than at Lavanya. She was convinced that Lavanya had a dubious past; claiming to be her aunt, Yogamaya had contrived a scheme to pass on Lavanya to Amit. It doesn't take rocket science to fool a man.

Cissie came forward, gave Yogamaya a slight greeting and said, 'I'm Cissie, Amit's sister.'

Yogamaya smiled. She said, 'Amit calls me Mashima, which gives me the right, my dear, to be an aunt to you as well.' Yogamaya was repulsed by Katie. She didn't take any notice of her. To Cissie, she said, 'Come, dear, come inside.'

'There is no time,' replied Cissie. 'I came only to inquire if Amit is here.'

'He hasn't come yet,' said Yogamaya.

'Do you know when he might come?'

'I can't say. But I'll find out.'

Without moving from her chair, Katie exclaimed, 'The schoolmistress who was coaching here pretended she had never met Amit.'

Yogamaya was dumbfounded. She sensed trouble. She realized that it would be difficult to maintain one's dignity around these people. Ignoring her position as an aunt, she remarked, 'I understand that Amit Babu has checked into your hotel. You should know where he is.'

Katie laughed loudly, as if to say, 'You may try to, but you can't fool us.'

The truth was that Katie had become angry and upset when Lavanya had said she didn't know who Amit was. Cissie, on the other hand, wasn't upset. She found Yogamaya's natural dignity attractive; she had been embarrassed when Katie refused to stand up to greet Yogamaya. However, she didn't dare to go against Katie, who mercilessly put down any of her friends who disagreed with her. She could be very rude and prided herself on her candour and frankness. In order to avoid her wrath, her friends did everything to please her, just to maintain the peace. Cissie belonged to this category of friends. The more scared she was of Katie, the more she agreed with her. This time, she didn't succeed. Katie realized that Cissie was uncomfortable with her rudeness and open defiance. She decided that these misgivings had to be crushed in Yogamaya's presence. She got up, thrust a cigarette in Cissie's mouth and pulled her towards herself to light the cigarette from the one that she was smoking. Cissie didn't dare to object, but her ears turned red in embarrassment. Katie wanted to show that she could ignore those who might frown at her Western ways.

Amit arrived at this juncture. The two women were taken aback. When Amit had left the hotel, he was dressed English-style, with a jacket, trousers and a felt hat. Now, he appeared in a dhoti, kurta and shawl. He had gone to his cottage from the hotel to change. The cottage comprised a shelf full of books, a dresser and an easy chair that Yogamaya had gifted him. After lunch at the hotel, he would go to his cottage and rest for a while. Lavanya was strict with her time. She didn't like any interruption when she would be tutoring Surama, until four-thirty in the afternoon. After this, she would meet Amit for tea. Amit had no choice but to follow this routine.

The ring had arrived from Calcutta this morning. How he would ceremoniously put the ring on Lavanya's finger had occupied Amit's mind all day. The day was special. All usual business had to be suspended. He had made up his mind to march straight to Lavanya and say, 'The king was on elephant back, the gate was low; rather than bending his head, he went back without entering the newly built palace. Today, the great moment of our life has arrived, but you have built your gate too low. Pull it down so that the king may enter with his head held high.' He had also thought of adding that to arrive at the right time might define punctuality, but what the watch said wasn't the true time. The watch might know the time, but how could it know its real worth?

Amit looked up. The sky was grey with clouds. Already,

the light of the day had dimmed. It seemed as if it was five or six in the afternoon, not four-thirty. Amit did not look at his watch. He had arrived early.

The area on the terrace where Lavanya sat to coach Surama was visible from the road. He noticed that it was empty. The thought that Lavanya had finished early cheered him. He looked at his watch. It was only three-twenty. The other day, he had told Lavanya that following rules was required of humans; not following them was the privilege of gods. On earth, we abide by the law so that while in heaven we may enjoy the pleasure of breaking the law. He hoped that Lavanya had finally appreciated the significance of breaking the law. Perhaps the power of the 'special day' had moved her.

Closer to the house, he noticed a shocked Yogamaya standing still while Cissie was lighting her cigarette from Katie's. The deliberate insult was apparent to everyone. Tabby, brushed aside by Katie, was lying next to her feet. As Amit approached, Tabby greeted him with his usual excitement. Cissie snapped, scolding the dog.

Amit ignored Cissie and Katie. 'Mashima,' he called out. He then bent down to touch her feet. It was rather unusual for him to do this at this time.

'Where is Lavanya?' he asked.

'I don't quite know. Perhaps she is in her room, my son.'

'It's not yet time for her to finish her teaching Surama.'

'I think she stopped when they arrived.'

'Let's go in and see what she is doing.' Amit entered the room with Yogamaya. He completely ignored the presence of Cissie and Katie.

'That's an insult!' cried Cissie. 'Let's go home, Katie.'

The slight had incensed Katie equally, but she wanted to see what would happen next.

'No use waiting,' said Cissie.

'Just wait,' answered Katie, fuming.

Time passed. Cissie implored again: 'Please, let us go. I don't feel like staying here one more minute.'

Katie wouldn't move away from the terrace. 'He must come out this way,' she said.

Amit came out at last, accompanied by Lavanya. She looked radiant and calm. There was no trace of resentment on her face. Yogamaya was inside the house. She wasn't feeling like coming out. Amit went in to get her. Katie noticed the ring on Lavanya's finger. She was furious.

'Mashima,' said Amit, 'this is my sister Samita. My father wanted my name to rhyme with hers, but it didn't quite work. And this is Ketaki, my sister's friend.'

In the meantime, another drama had been building up. Surama's pet cat had come out. This impertinent act seemed to Tabby's canine logic sufficient cause for him to challenge her to a fight. First, he growled. Then, he stared at the raised paws of the cat and became doubtful as to the outcome of the combat. Finally, standing at a sufficient distance, he decided that non-violent aggression would be the safest expression of heroism; he launched into a volley of barks. The cat ignored the barking. She simply walked past, arching her back high. This was too much for Katie. Enraged, she began to box Tabby's ears. Some of this was directed at her own fate, metaphorically speaking. Fate laughed in silence.

When the uproar was over, Amit turned to Cissie. 'Cissie, this is Lavanya. I've not mentioned her name to you before, but I believe you've heard it from many others. We are engaged. We will be married in Calcutta in November.'

Katie managed to smile. 'Congratulations! The orange orchard was not difficult to access after all. Nor was the road rough. The orange honey seems to have leapt into your mouth.'

Cissie giggled. Lavanya sensed the sarcasm in Katie's words, but she didn't understand what was being said. Amit explained: 'This morning, as I was walking out, they asked me where I was headed to. I replied that I was going in search of wild honey. That's what they are laughing at. It is my fault. Others cannot understand when I am serious and when I am simply joking.'

'Now that you have won your orange honey,' said Katie in a calm voice, 'you must see to it that I don't lose my bet.'

'What must I do?'

'I made a bet with Naren. No one can take you where men go—to the races. I bet my diamond ring that I will persuade you to take me to the races. I looked for you at all the waterfalls and all the honey stalls in town until I found you here. Didn't we look all over, Cissie, on a wild goose chase as they say in English?'

Cissie giggled some more.

'It reminds me of the story you once told me, Amit,' Katie went on. 'About a Russian philosopher. When his turban was stolen and he couldn't find it, he went and sat by a graveyard. For, said he, eventually he must come here. I was really surprised when Miss Lavanya said that she didn't know Amit, but something told me that, in the end, he would have to come to this graveyard of yours.'

Cissie laughed even more.

'Amit didn't mention your name,' Katie said to Lavanya. 'He talked in honey-soaked metaphors about orange honey. You are simple-witted, metaphors are too much for you, you can't turn the tricks of language. You simply blurted out that you didn't know Amit Raiye. The Sunday school dictum didn't work—neither of you received any punishment. One of you can tap the hard-to-get nectar and gulp it down. I'm apparently the only one without luck. I've lost my bet to Naren. How unfair, Cissie!'

Cissie laughed louder—no, the loudest! Even Tabby imagined that social etiquette called for his participation in this hilarity. He began fidgeting. For the third time, he had to be snubbed.

Katie said, 'If I lose this diamond ring, I shall never have peace. You had given it to me. I have not taken it off even once! It has become a part of me. It will be lost now, after all these years, on a bet in Shillong.'

'What made you go betting this, dear?' asked Cissie.

'I had pride in myself, and trust in men. Well, pride goes before a fall. I have lost my race and my bet. It seems I can no longer please Amit. Why did you give me the ring in the first place, with such affection, if you were going to finally jilt me like this? Was there no bond of love in this gift? A promise that you would never let me down?'

Katie was choking with emotion; with great effort, she held back her tears.

It had happened seven years ago, when Katie was eighteen. One day, Amit had taken off the ring from his finger and put it on hers. They were both in England then. A young Punjabi at Oxford was head over heels in love with Katie. That day, he and Amit had had a friendly rowing match on the river; Amit had won. The June moonlight had shone eloquently in the sky, bright blossoms were rioting in the meadows, hiding the earth underneath them. Amit had slipped the ring on to Katie's finger. Much had been implied, but there was no secret. Katie didn't plaster her face with make-up in those days, her laugh was natural and spontaneous, and she could still blush. As he had slipped the ring on her finger, Amit had whispered: *Tender is the night/And haply the queen moon is on her throne.*

Katie didn't talk much those days. She had taken a deep breath and murmured to herself, 'Mon ami!'

Now, even Amit had no answer. He didn't know what to say. Katie went on: 'Since I have lost the bet, Amit, you had better keep the ring as a token of my defeat. I won't let it lie on my finger.'

She took the ring off, put it on the table and hurried out. A torrent of tears poured down her enamelled cheeks.

16

Towards the Last Poem

A BRIEF LETTER reached Lavanya. It was from Shobhanlal.

'I arrived in Shillong last night. I would like to call on you, if you would not mind. If not, I shall leave tomorrow. I feel that you have punished me, but I am yet to understand why. I want to see you to find out, otherwise I shall have no peace of mind. Do not fear, I have no favour to ask.'

Lavanya's eyes welled up. She thought of the past in silence. She thought of her youthful fear that crushed the tender love. All this time, it had had room to grow and blossom, but she had been too proud of her learning and knowledge, her sense of independence, of being free. She had taken pride in her father's wisdom and considered love unnecessary and irrelevant. Now, love had taken root, her vanity had gone. What could have been natural and spontaneous was now most difficult to face. It was not easy to welcome a person from a past long gone. Yet, it was difficult to turn him away. She remembered the face of a deeply hurt and pained Shobhanlal. How had the young man's infatuation still survived?

Lavanya wrote: 'You're the best friend I have ever had. I have nothing to offer that can repay your friendship. You, of course, never wanted anything in return. You made no claims. I do not have the vanity or pride to turn you away. Please come.'

Soon after she sent the letter, Amit arrived. 'Come, Vanya,' he said. 'Let us go out.' He spoke rather timidly, fearing that Lavanya would say no. However, she simply said, 'Let us go.'

Amit held Lavanya's hand as they went out. He held it tight. He didn't have words to express his feelings. Walking along, they arrived at a glade they had visited before. The sun went down behind the crest of trees. The green of the trees blended with the blue of the sky. They stopped.

Lavanya spoke gently: 'Why did you offer me the ring that you had given to someone else?'

Amit looked hurt. 'How can I explain to you, Vanya, that the person I had offered the ring to once is not the same any more?'

'Look, Mita, the one who had completely surrendered to you, why didn't you fully accept her?'

'That is not quite correct. I'm not responsible for what Katie is today.'

'But she once gave herself to you, Mita. Why didn't you make her your own? You refused her hand of friendship.

Since then, she has offered it to a dozen others, and that has made her what she is. It was because she lost you that she made herself up to attract others. She looks like a decorated, fake English doll now. It wouldn't have happened if she could have had you. All right, let us not talk about it any more. I want to ask you for a favour, and you must say yes.'

'Of course I will. What is it?'

'Take your friends on a trip to Cherrapunjee for a few days. Even though you can't make her happy, you can offer her some enjoyment.'

After some hesitation, Amit said, 'All right.'

Lavanya put her head on Amit's chest and said, 'I'm going to say something, Mita, which I'll not say again. The bond between us doesn't bind you anyway. I'm saying this with love. Please don't give me any ring. Our love doesn't need any token to prove it. Let it remain completely untainted by a material thing.'

She took the ring from her finger and put it on Amit's. Amit did not resist.

In the radiant twilight, Lavanya looked at Amit.

After a few days in Cherrapunjee, Amit went to Yogamaya's house. The house was locked. There was no one inside. Amit stood under the familiar eucalyptus tree, then he began to pace around. The gardener came and asked, 'Shall I open the house? Would you like to go in?'

'Yes,' replied Amit, after a slight hesitation.

He went to Lavanya's room. The desk, the chair and the shelf were there, but the books were missing. On the floor, a few envelopes, with Lavanya's name and address written in an unfamiliar hand, were lying around. Two or three discarded pens lay on the desk. Amit put one of them in his pocket. In the adjacent bedroom, there was a mattress on the bedstead and an empty bottle of oil. Amit threw himself on the mattress, his head buried between his hands. The iron bed creaked. The room was filled with a silent emptiness; it couldn't answer Amit's questions.

Amit went to his cottage. He was tired and listless. Everything was there just as he had left it. The easy chair was there, Yogamaya had not taken it back. He appreciated the fact that it had been given to him with much affection, as a gift. He could almost hear her voice, her sweet voice. Amit put his forehead on the chair respectfully, in obeisance.

The hills of Shillong had lost their charm for Amit. He couldn't find peace anywhere.

17

The Last Poem

YATISHANKAR WAS IN college in Calcutta—he was
attending Presidency College. He stayed in its hostel at
Kalutola. Amit occasionally took him home for dinner
and for drives in his car. He liked shocking Yati with his
irreverent remarks on things.

Then, for some time, Yatishankar did not see Amit. He
heard he had gone to Nainital, or maybe Ootacamund.
One day, he heard that a friend of Amit's had said in jest
that Amit had lately been busy taking the enamel off
Katie Mitter's face. He had finally found a job to his
liking: changing colours! So far, Amit had fulfilled his
creative passion with words; now, he had found a live
human being to recreate. As for the concerned human
being, she too was removing the painted petals from her
face. Lissie remarked that Katie had changed beyond
recognition—she was looking like her natural self. She

had even asked her friends to begin calling her Ketaki instead of Katie. This was like overdressing a woman who would earlier display her curves in light, gossamer fabric. Amit was apparently calling her Keya in private. It was rumoured that on Nainital lake, Katie had taken control of the oars as Amit read out Tagore's 'Aimless Journey' to her. But people talk and tattle—Yati figured that Amit's mind had been swept away in the high tide of the holiday spirit.

Amit was back. It was rumoured that he and Ketaki were engaged to be married, although Amit himself had said nothing to that effect to Yati. Amit's manners had undoubtedly changed. He still brought English books to Yati, but he no longer spent evenings discussing them. Yati could understand that Amit's passions had now found a new outlet. Amit did not invite Yati out for a ride in his car any longer. It was not hard for Yati to figure out that in Amit's 'Aimless Journey', there was no room for a third person.

Yati could not restrain himself any longer. He asked Amit point blank: 'Amitda, I hear you are engaged to marry Miss Ketaki Mitter?'

After a moment's pause, Amit asked in return: 'Has Lavanya heard that?'

'No, I have not written to her. I wouldn't do that without checking with you first.'

'The news is true, but I'm afraid Lavanya will misunderstand.'

Yati laughed. 'What is there to misunderstand? If you marry, you marry. Simple enough.'

'Look, Yati, what people say is never simple. A word may have only one straight meaning according to the dictionary, but it assumes many meanings as people talk. It's like the Ganga forking out in multiple streams when it nears the sea.'

'In other words,' remarked Yati, 'you mean to suggest that marriage doesn't mean marriage.'

'What I'm saying is that marriage has a thousand meanings. It assumes its many meanings in different lives. You eliminate lives from it, and the meaning is confused.'

'Well, let us have your definition then.'

'It cannot be defined. It has to be lived. If I say that, in essence, it means love, I run into another problematic word. The thing called love is more dynamic than the thing called marriage.'

'In that case, Amitda, there will be an end to all discussion. Are we to go chasing the meaning under a load of words while it swerves left or right as it pleases? One cannot go on like that.'

'Well said! My teaching has inspired you to ask good questions. Words are essential to carry on our work in the world. Truths that are too big for words have to be made simple—it is the words that count. What else can we do? It may be intellectually unsatisfactory, but we must get on with the job.'

'Do we then forget discussion?'

'No harm in that, if it is only an intellectual exercise, without any vital connection to life.'

'Well, let us assume that there is a vital connection.'

'Hear, hear! Then listen.'

A brief comment is relevant here. These days Yati comes here for a cup of tea served by Amit's youngest sister Lissie. It is obvious that is the reason Yati did not mind that lately Amit wasn't engaging him in literary discourse in the afternoon or inviting him for a drive in the evening. He had forgiven Amit with all his heart.

Amit said, 'Oxygen is invisibly present in the air, otherwise life couldn't exist. It also reunites with the coal in the fire, which we put to so many uses. In neither form can we do without it. Do you understand now?'

'Not quite, though I would like to.'

'Love that freely floats in the sky is our soul; love that informs our daily life illumines our homes. I want both of them!'

'I have no idea whether I understand you. Could you be a little more explicit?'

Amit said, 'There is a day when I can spread my wings and reach the heavens; then, I find my little home, where I lie in my little nest with my wings folded. But I still have my heaven.'

'Can't these two meet in marriage?'

'Happy coincidences are possible, but they rarely happen. He is lucky who wins the princess and half the kingdom together. But the man who holds the kingdom by the right hand and the princess by the left, is a pretty lucky fellow indeed.'

'But—'

'But does it suffer in what you call romance? Not a bit. Must we model our romances after the novels? By no means. I'll invent my romance. One will flourish in my heaven; the other on earth. You'll call them romantic, those who try to save one over the other. They must either swim in the water like fish, or pace the riverbank like cats, or wander about in the air like owls. I am the prophet of romance. I shall realize the truth of love on land and air as well as in the sky. The islet in the river will hold my home; then I shall reach out to the sky as well. Long live my Lavanya! Long live my Ketaki. And blessed in every respect will be Amit Ray!'

Yati sat silently. It was not clear to him whether he relished the idea. Amit smiled at his confusion. 'Look, Yati, one man's meat is another man's poison. What I'm saying need only to apply to myself. If you make it your own, you'll misunderstand and will only blame me. There is strife in the world every time one man foists his meaning on another man's words. Let me now explain further. I'll use a metaphor instead of an actual word. What binds me to Ketaki is love, but this love is like water in a vessel. I'll draw it, and use it every day. My love for Lavanya is like a lake, which can't be brought home in a vessel. My mind will swim in it.'

Yati asked with hesitation, 'But Amitda, couldn't we have a choice between the two?'

'Those who can may, but I can't.'

'But if Miss Ketaki—'

'She knows everything. Whether she understands it completely, I cannot say. I shall spend my whole life telling her that I have not deceived her. She must know too that she is in Lavanya's debt.'

'That's all right. But Miss Lavanya must be told that you're planning to marry someone else.'

'Without fail. But before that, I want to send a letter. Will you take it to her?'

'Of course.'

Amit wrote: 'That day, when we stood at the end of the road, I ended our journey with a poem. It cannot be expressed in words. Poor Nivaran died the day he was caught, like a most delicate fish. Since there is thus no choice, I turn to your favourite poet Tagore to speak to you for me.'

Invisible, you're unchanging in my eyes.
In the unseen chamber of heart
You'll reside forever.
I've found the stone that turns all into gold,
You've filled the great void in me.
Life was darkness when I saw in my heart
The lighted lamp you left as your parting gift,
Separation, like sacred fire burned in glow
In love's sorrow.

Days passed. Ketaki had gone to attend the annaprashan—the 'first meal' ceremony—of her sister's infant daughter. Amit did not go. Ensconced in an easy chair, he was reading the letters of William James. Yati brought him a letter from Lavanya. On one side of the letter was the announcement of Lavanya's wedding to Shobhanlal, six months later, in June, on the Ramgarh Hills. On the other side, it said:

Are you in tune with Time?
The wheels of its journey
Stir gaping wounds of wail
In darkness,
And the heart wakes up in fear.
Dear friend, these ruthless wheels
Have taken me away from your side,
And flung me far away,
Across a thousand deaths
On the peak of a strange dawn.

I was whirled away in the storm of Time,
No way is left for return.
You would not know me now,
Farewell, my friend.

Yet on an idle day in Spring
The fallen bakul flowers
Moan to the sky,
A sigh from the forgotten past
Rustles through your being.
Maybe, if you look within
You'll find a bit of me
In the twilight, shaping a nameless dream.

No, not a dream!
The supreme truth of love,
My love, death-conquering,
My gift to you is imperishable, unchanging.
Let me be borne away
By the changing tide—

The gift remains.
Farewell, my friend.

No loss is yours in losing me,
An image of clay.
If of that mortal dust
You've fashioned a goddess,
Let it stay with you with the evening star.
No touch shall disturb
The play of your offering,
No hot breath will sully the flowers.

To the rich repast of your imagination
I shall not come with my bowl
Wet with hungry tears.
Who knows, you may fashion with words,
Out of fragments
Of what remains of me
In your memory,
That weight stays not as a burden
Nor makes any claims.
Farewell, my friend.

Grieve not on my account,
Wide is the world with many tasks.
My cup is not discarded
Shall fill again—
Let this sustain me forever.
I may yet be blessed
If there be one eager heart
Waiting for my footsteps.
I long to give myself to him

Who can see in the compassion of love
The actual me, a blend of good and ill
Who can light up the dark night
With flowers plucked in moonlight.

What I gave to you is yours
By everlasting right.
What others receive
Are daily driblets of heart
To tender solitude.
O my peerless friend,
What I gave you was your own gift—
Fuller acceptance, the deeper my debt.
Farewell, my friend.

Bangalore
25 June 1928

A Note on
Rabindranath Tagore

Translator's Note

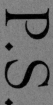

Insights
Interviews &
More ...

A Note on Rabindranath Tagore

Dilip Basu

Author, activist, artist, choreographer, dramatist, educator, musician and philosopher, Rabindranath Tagore (1861–1941) was primarily a poet. He was called a 'Universal Man', which he certainly was. His roots, both cultural and creative, were set deep in his beloved Bengal. His talents blossomed from the dusty and wet plains of Bengal in over a thousand poems, two-and-a-half thousand songs, a sizeable number of short stories, novels, and discursive essays on education, history, literature, rural reconstruction, politics, philosophy and science. He became a painter rather late in his life, when he turned seventy. In ten years, he produced approximately three thousand paintings.

Tagore was born in the Jorasanko District of Kolkata on 7 May 1861. He was the youngest child of Debendranath Tagore (1817–1905) and Sarada Devi (1826–1875). Originally from Jessore (now in Bangladesh), the Tagore (Thakur in Bengali) family belonged to a Brahmin sub-caste known as Pirali. Orthodox Brahmins refused to maintain any social contact with the Tagores and Piralis due to their closeness to Muslim rulers. The family moved to Kolkata in the 1690s – around the time the city was founded. The Tagores prospered, working for the East India Company. Rabindranath's grandfather, Dwarkanath Tagore (1794–1846), known as 'the Prince', built the family fortune with his great enterprises, including banking, insurance, agency houses, mining, shipping and real estate. A contemporary of Rammohan Roy (1772–1833) and a close associate of his in the social reform movement, Dwarkanath was arguably India's first modern and global entrepreneur. His industrial enterprises collapsed soon after he passed away, but the extensive landed estates he had built up in East Bengal continued to comfortably support the extended family in the next generation.

Debendranath Tagore's large family lived in a commodious mansion in Jorasanko. All his children distinguished themselves in some way or the other. Dwijendranath Tagore (1840–1926) was a poet and philosopher, Satyendranath Tagore (1842–1923) was the first Indian to join the Indian Civil Service, Jyotirindranath (1849–1925) was a playwright and translator, and Swarnakumari Devi (1855–1925) was India's first woman novelist.

As a child, Rabindranath had trouble studying in school. He disliked the set curriculum, the strict discipline and the restrictive atmosphere of the four schools he attended until he was thirteen. He was withdrawn from St. Xavier's School in 1874. Thereafter, he received schooling at home from his brother Jyotirindranath and Jyotirindranath's wife Kadambari Devi. Both of them exercised great influence on Rabindranath's literary pursuits during his adolescence and early adult life.

Tagore began to publish verse, narrative poetry, short fiction and translation from 1876 onwards in the family's literary journal *Bharati*. He also started to act on the family stage. He appeared, for example, in the title role of Molière's *Le Bourgeois Gentilhomme*, adapted into a Bengali farce by Jyotirindranath. The following year, he travelled to London with Satyendranath. He enrolled at the University College, London, to read English literature. His frankly explicit 'letters' from London alarmed his elders, who felt concerned about his youthful waywardness. He received urgent summons to return home. Upon reaching Kolkata, he began to publish in earnest. His opera *Valmiki Pratibha* (*The Genius of*

Valmiki), modelled after the European operas he had seen in London, impressed Kolkata's literary elites, especially those engaged in experimenting with Western literary genres and music. Tagore scored the music for the opera and cast himself in the title role. He recorded his first major poetic inspiration in a passionate work titled 'The Awakening of the Waterfall' ('Nirjharer Swapnabhanga'), and a plethora of new works followed. This included a series of devotional songs in the tradition of the medieval Mithila Vaisnava poet Vidyapati. He composed these songs in the company of Kadambari Devi, his talented sister-in-law.

In 1883, Tagore had an arranged marriage with Mrinalini Devi. The next year, Kadambari Devi committed suicide, apparently due to her unrequited love for Rabindranath. The tragedy shattered Tagore and arguably created the emotional impetus for his novella *Nashtanir* (*The Broken Nest*), which Satyajit Ray adapted for his film *Charulata* (1964). By 1890, when Tagore visited England again, he was considered a top literary talent in Bengal by no less an author than Bankim Chandra Chatterjee, the then doyen of Bengali letters.

Tagore spent the next decade (1890–1900) supervising the family's extensive landed estates in what is now Bangladesh. The experience brought him in close and intimate contact with Bengal's countryside and its people. He wrote scores of short stories showing the dark side of Bengal's village life while celebrating in exquisite verse the beauty and bounty of the land.

The first decade of the twentieth century saw the emergence of two diametrically opposed profiles of Tagore: the first was that of a dedicated patriot and political activist, and the second that of a deeply mystical poet searching for unity and oneness in the complexity and diversity of the universe.

Tagore's political involvement had begun in 1886, when he composed and sang at the inauguration of the Indian National

Congress. The next year, he participated in the public protest against the blatantly discriminatory policies of Lord Cross, the secretary of state for India. One sees Tagore's fully formed political personality and activism in the wake of Lord Curzon's decision in 1905 to partition the province of Bengal into two halves, roughly corresponding to the Hindu and Muslim populations. The Swadeshi (self-rule) movement (1905–11) was the first major 'militant' agitation against colonial rule. During the first phase, Tagore led the protestors in the streets of Kolkata, singing patriotic songs he had composed for the movement. He gave music to Bankim Chatterjee's famous hymn to the motherland, 'Vande Mataram', which soon became the battle cry of the anti-partition patriots and the name of a fiery journal edited by Aurobindo Ghose (later Sri Aurobindo). Terror and violence marked the extremist challenge against the Raj in Bengal. Unable to accept the narrow nationalism and its destructive divisiveness, Tagore withdrew himself from the movement, and was quickly condemned and criticized. Some called him a 'lackey' of the British. A decade later, in 1915, Tagore published Ghare Baire (The Home and the World), a major novel (also later adapted into a film by Satyajit Ray) in which he articulated his thesis on nationalism.

This period of intense public activism was followed by private withdrawal, which coincided with great personal tragedies in Tagore's life. His wife Mrinalini passed away in 1902, his daughter Renuka died in 1903, and so did his father Debendranath in 1905, and in 1907 his youngest son Samindranath died of cholera. It appears that Tagore attempted to negotiate the many crises in a series of profoundly moving poems, also songs, uniting humanity to nature and vice versa. His own elegant yet simple prose translation of Gitanjali took the English literary circles by storm in 1912. Among Tagore's admirers in England were Mez Sinclair, Evelyn Underhill, Ezra Pound, Bertrand Russell, and most importantly, W.B. Yeats, the Irish poet. 'These prose translations from Rabindranath Tagore have stirred my blood as nothing has for years,' Yeats wrote in his introduction to *Gitanjali*.[1] In 1912–13, Tagore was in the United States lecturing at Chicago, Urbana, Rochester and Harvard. Soon after his return to India, he received the news that he had been awarded the Nobel Prize in Literature.

Yeats lamented that even though the poetry of Tagore stirred sublime emotions in him, he knew nothing about 'his life, and of the movements of thought that have made them possible'. At once unique to Bengal and universal, Tagore's work was the product of the Anglo-Bengali, East–West encounters of the nineteenth century. The colonial world Tagore inhabited and the asymmetrical power relations among the colonizers and the colonized prompted him to seek new and novel ways to express his autonomy and creativity.

Over the next thirty years, one can locate this dialectical process in three areas of Tagore's life. The first was the project of building a utopian community in Santiniketan, 100 miles outside Kolkata in the saffron-coloured soil of southern Bengal. In 1863, Debendranath had bought some land and built a great house and named it Santiniketan (abode of peace). A prayer hall was built in 1891. In 1901, Rabindranath established an academic institution to provide an 'overall development of the students amidst close contact with nature . . . classes were to be held in open air under the shades of the trees'.[2] In 1918, Tagore transformed the institution into Visva-Bharati (World University). Although the atmosphere and environment reminded one of the communities of the Upanishadic age of the pre-Christian era, Visva-Bharati was purportedly a

---

1. W.B. Yeats, 'Introduction to Rabindranath Tagore', *Gitanjali*, New York: Dover Publications, 2000, unabridged edition, p. ix

2. T.K. Basak, *Rabindranath, Santiniketan, Sriniketan*, Bolpur: B.B. Publications, 2004, pp. 1–5

twentieth-century academy. Tagore invited scholars and students from the East and the West to occupy an academic and creative space that was, by design and intent, outside the baneful influences of colonialism, industrialism and nationalism. To raise funds for Visva-Bharati and to speak about its mission, he travelled the globe: to China and Japan (1924), South America (1925), Europe and Egypt (1926), South-East Asia (1927) and Canada (1929). He delivered the Hibbert Lectures at Oxford in 1930, which were published as *Religion of Man*.

Tagore attempted to provide a practical and material foundation to his vision of the World University. At the adjacent Sriniketan, he established the Centre for Rural Reconstruction in 1922. Its first director was Leonard K. Elmhirst, an English agricultural expert. Experimental research activities accompanied agronomy and rural development. Chemical fertilizers and modern medical facilities were introduced. The focus at Sriniketan was, and still is, on vocational education: leather craft, woodcraft, clay craft, lacquer work, embroidery, bookbinding, carpet weaving, and block carving and printing. Along with the Art School (Kala Bhavana) and the Music School (Sangit Bhavana), the Santiniketan–Sriniketan complex combined the practice of the traditional arts with contemporary and modern elements.

The second project that preoccupied Tagore during this period concerned his scrupulous spurring of forms of colonial knowledge, and his staunch anti-imperialist and anti-nationalist positions. He rejected, for example, 'academic histories' that are narrowly focused on political and public policies of the state. In numerous poems, plays and novels, he attempted to capture what Ranajit Guha has called 'historicality' of everyday life.[3]

---

3. Ranajit Guha, *History at the Limit of World History*, New York: Columbia University Press, 2002, pp. 74–76

Tagore surrendered his knighthood in an angry protest against the Jallianwala Bagh massacre of 1919. Although he disagreed with Gandhi about some aspects of the nationalist movement, his harshest criticism was directed at the West, sundered as it was by the Holocaust and World War II. In his last address and testament to the world before he passed away in 1941, he stated, 'Perhaps the new dawn will come from this horizon, from the East where the sun rises.'[4]

The third area of Tagore's involvement was his continued creative effort. He remained magnificently innovative and profusely productive to his last day. He started experimenting with *vers libre* in 1933; he invented a new form of drama combining music, mime and dance. He took up painting at seventy, and the three thousand paintings he completed are considered among the best of modern Indian art.

William Radice, arguably the best translator of Tagore in English, divides Tagore's life and work into a series of paired oppositions borrowed from *Isha Upanishad*: he moves, he moves not; he is far, he is near; he is within all, and he is outside all. Tagore moved away from the orthodox Brahmo church founded by his father; he also moved away from Hindu revivalism and nationalism. Tagore was quite a radical in more ways than one, but he remained tradition-bound in some key areas. For example, he married a ten-year-old semi-literate girl from his own caste, and followed the family custom by getting his two daughters married when they were only twelve and fourteen.

Tagore can prove utterly foreign to non-Bengali readers. Although there are some good translations, most of his poetry is inadequate, if not inaccessible, in translation. His songs are a good example.

---

4. Rabindranath Tagore, *Crisis in Civilization*, Kolkata: Visva Bharati Press, 1942, pp.12–13

There are over two-and-a-half thousand of them, sung and listened to every day by Bengalis everywhere. As a composer of songs, Satyajit Ray says that Tagore has no equal even in the West.[5] Most non-Bengalis, however, are denied the pleasure of enjoying Tagore's songs. Yet, he is, in his fervent idealism, in his spiritual reality, in his romanticism, near to all of humankind. Tagore's modernity as a poet, thinker and activist is accessible to most, as are his anti-materialist, feminist and educational ideals. Most important is the agency or autonomy of Tagore the artist and poet, and its expression in creative work. His personality and life are present in his poetry, plays, stories and novels. He is within all. Yet he is outside all. Human creativity is, in his own words, 'amoral, arbitrary, fanciful, whimsical, unreal', and the natural artist in him 'is naughty, good for nothing, separate from the man of a hundred good intentions'.[6]

Is it possible to overcome the translational problems to appreciate Tagore the poet? Anna Akhmatova, who translated Tagore into Russian, offers an insight: 'He is a great poet, I can see that now. It's not only a matter of individual lines which have real genius, or individual poems . . . but that mighty flow of poetry which takes its strength from Hinduism as from the Ganges, and is called Rabindranath Tagore.'[7]

5. Quoted in Krishna Dutta and Andrew Robinson, *Rabindranath Tagore: An Anthology*, London: Picador, 1999, p. 385

6. Ibid., pp. 36–37

7. Ibid., p. 1

Translator's Note

In January 1928, Rabindranath Tagore was in Colombo, Sri Lanka, on his way to England where he had been invited to deliver the Hibbert Lectures at Oxford University. Unfortunately, he fell ill while in Colombo and decided to return to India. He arrived in Bangalore to rest for three weeks at the home of Sir Brajendranath Seal, the philosopher who was at the time the vice chancellor of Mysore University.

During his brief sojourn in Bangalore, he finished writing *Shesher Kavita* which he had begun while in Colombo.

The intensely romantic plot of *Shesher Kavita* unfolds in Shillong, the beautiful hill station in north-east India. Tagore had visited Shillong thrice: in 1919, 1923 and 1927. He spent a month and a half in Shillong in 1923. At that time, he was sixty-two but quite youthful, and very romantic at heart. The idea of writing a novel saturated with love, romance and poetry, and set in Shillong naturally occurred to him. Amitrasudan Bhattacharya, the noted scholar of Bengali literature, has concluded that the maverick hero of *Shesher Kavita*, Amit Ray, was none other than Tagore himself. He was seen walking every afternoon with a seventeen-year-old young woman, Ranu Adhikari (later Lady Ranu Mukherjee). There are about 250 letters that Tagore had written to Ranu Adhikari till she got married to Sir Birendranath Mukherjee, the noted industrialist. The relationship was one of considerable mutual affection; whether it had blossomed into a romantic one in the metonymic sense, as suggested by Bhattacharya, remains a moot point. It is, however, conceivable that Tagore modelled the character of Lavanya in *Shesher Kavita* after Ranu; whether Amit Ray in the novel is Tagore himself will be stretching the comparison a bit too far. Tagore presents himself in the novel as a butt of Amit's trenchant criticism. He is quoted as saying that the strongest objection to Tagore is 'imitating Wordsworth, he insists most perversely on continuing' to write poetry at the age of sixty-two.

Shesher Kavita remains unique not only in Tagore's magnificent oeuvre but also in all of Bengali literature, perhaps even in world literature. It is almost poetry that only Tagore could write to illuminate and enliven the narrative; it is playful, satirical and sad. It has charming and challenging dialogues; it is witty and wise, and set in the picturesque hills of Shillong. It ends on a tragic note, voiced in a beautiful poem, which lends itself to the title of the book *Shesher Kavita, The Last Poem*.

The novel is difficult to put down once one starts reading it. I hope this immensely pleasurable aspect of reading this masterpiece comes through in the present translation too. I have followed the original novel as far as possible while trying to maintain its readability in English.

I thank Keya Ganguly and Ram Ray for reading the translation and offering valuable suggestions. Prasenjit Das Gupta and Soumen Paul have provided help with material concerning the publication of *Shesher Kavita* in 1928 and thereafter. I am grateful to Suresh Kohli for suggesting that I submit this manuscript to HarperCollins India for publication, and to Shantanu Ray Chaudhuri at HarperCollins India for enthusiastically accepting it.

I am immensely indebted to Dinkar Kowshik, who unfortunately did not live to see this translation published, for beautifully illustrating it with twelve colour sketches. Some of these have appeared in a recent Bengali edition of the book. In fact, the illustrations inspired me to undertake the translation.

I am much appreciative of Dayani Kowshik's interest in this project, and for her help in scanning Dinkar Kowshik's illustrations. Dayani told me stories about Krishna Kripalini, the first translator of *Shesher Kavita*, whom she had known during her childhood. My daughter Amiya, always interested in what I do, regularly inquired about the progress of the translation. Dayani and my student assistant Charlotte Floyd patiently typed as well as made suggestions to the manuscript from my handwritten version. I thank them.

This translation of *Shesher Kavita* is my tribute to Rabindranath Tagore on his 150th birth anniversary this year.